I.O.T.A.A

WHEN YOU WANT TO TRAVEL THE WORLD,
CONTACT A TRAVEL AGENT. WHEN YOU
WANT TO TRAVEL THE UNIVERSE, CONTACT
I.O.T.A.A.

MARYELLEN HUNTER

This is a work of fiction. names, characters, businesses, places, events, locales, and incidents are either the products of the author's imagination or used in a fictitious manner. Any resemblance to actual persons, living or dead, or actual events is purely coincidental.

ISBN: 979-8-9859548-4-5 (paperback)
ISBN: 979-8-9859548-5-2 (digital)

DEDICATION

To my 'Space Case' son Marcus,
for his steadfast encouragement.

As Earth technology melded with the vastly advanced shared knowledge of interplanetary visitors, the Earth was included in the development of teleportation centers providing the ability to quickly travel to other "Earth Class" planets throughout the universe.

Each of these planets offered unique opportunities to entice visitors. The guest travelers who could afford the cost of escaping the crowded planets from which they came were not disappointed until they discovered the irony of their dreams coming true.

The teleportation systems were controlled by a group of intergalactic lifeforms who identified their consortium as the Intergalactic Operational Transport Authority Agency.

EROS

How excited Angie was, she had finally been accepted to move to Eros and rejoin her husband, James. They had longed to have children but were prevented from realizing that dream on Earth. The tests to determine their fertility ratings had cost them their life savings, but they had each continued working to save more for the opportunity to be 'transported' to Eros. I.O.T.A.A. had approved the Eros destination as the planet where fertility was assured, and reproductive restrictions were non-existent. The vegetation there contained nutrients not yet available on Earth. These nutrients stimulated the human body to produce more resilient sperm in males and extend the years of egg production in females. More importantly, this growing planet's managers enthusiastically welcomed those seeking to produce offspring and increase the planet's population.

Living on Earth, where unapproved reproduction was a global offense, most women passed the childbearing age before their applications to bear children were ever approved. In her case, Angie was getting close to forty-five, so the Eros destination was their only hope to leave the crowded and restricted planet. She would occasionally receive communications from her husband on Eros. They were a bit sterile in the verbiage and unlike him. The rare bits he did write indicated that he had radically increased fertility and expressed confidence that they could look forward to being happy parents. He did express his pleasure at her having received final approval to join him, which served to bolster her enthusiasm.

Those communications were a welcome distraction from the thoughts of missing her mother. If her mother hadn't died last year, she would have received the news of Angie's ability to finally have children with both joy and sadness. Joy in hearing the news that she would have grandchildren, but sadness knowing she would never see the children born on another planet. She would, however, have been comforted with the knowledge that her grandchildren would not have to grow up on Earth with its crowds, crime and restrictions.

Angie had been part of a group of wives, in the same position, waiting to qualify for permission to bear a child. Some of the women discovered fertility issues that inhibited the process, frequently beyond the time and capability to conceive. Many of this group had given up businesses and homes to fund their move to Eros. A few had even communicated their joy at starting their families on Eros.

Some of the remaining group members suggested that the content of the E-comms from EROS seemed a bit impersonal or contrived. Angie ignored these comments, assuming that they were being malicious or jealous. She decided that these women, who had moved, were probably so busy raising their babies that there was no time for long descriptive narratives about their joys on Eros. Angie chose to be optimistic, once she got to Eros and conceived, she was committed to writing lengthy heartfelt tales of her joy. She planned to encourage the remaining Earth members of this group.

She had considered writing to tell her husband how very

happy she was to have received her departure date for the GaliPort. But at this point, she was just too excited about closing this chapter of her life to be able to coherently describe how she was feeling. She knew the two-month-long series of health and psychological tests would probably keep her busy when she arrived, but he would understand as he must surely have experienced the same protocol ten months ago when he arrived there. I.O.T.A.A. had assured her that the approval and transport date would be communicated to him, and he would be waiting for her on Eros once her arrival testing was completed. She questioned if the arrival testing would take another two months, but they assured her that the testing was more immunological in nature, due to the movement through the time/space continuum. They assured her that it was unrelated to the earlier fertility testing, and very much focused on the safety and protection of the entire society on Eros.

Angie had some great friends at her apartment building and her job. Most would be happy to hear her news, but sad that their friend was leaving, and some would be jealous that they would be staying behind. For others, her departure would be an opportunity to possibly advance their careers through the vacated position. The landlord would be pleased as he would be able to start a bidding war with prospective new tenants to occupy the soon-to-be empty location.

It was time to go to the I.O.T.A.A. meeting where her final questions would be answered, and preparation instructions would be provided. The documentation about the actual teleport process was complicated but it clearly stated that no traveler was permitted to take earth possessions with them. It had been explained thoroughly, months ago, but she wanted to be refreshed in the details again because back then, it was a dream, now it was real.

She dressed in her newest uniform for the meeting and off she went. Three transport tube transfers later, she arrived at the I.O.T.A.A. office in the heart of Atlanta. It was an imposing building that towered above the surrounding skyscrapers in all directions. The collection of buildings effectively blocked the sun. The steel and mirrored glass architecture seemed to touch the sky, while the walls of glass reflected images of the hundreds of people moving about it. The images were repeated in each and every window giving the optical illusion of a continuous march of thousands. As she looked at the sea of people on the building wall, she tried to guess how many floors were in the building, but it was impossible. Trying to count the rows of windows always ended in being distracted by the hordes of people crossing each panel and her attempt caused a sense of vertigo. Suddenly she realized she was standing there staring at images she would never see again once she left to rejoin her husband.

Returning from her reverie, she quickly moved forward to the main door. Entering the building, she was surprised by the instantaneous quiet. The silence was as unsettling as staring at the crowds and images outside had been. Outside she had been surrounded by an endless din that she had lived with her entire life. Now the din was gone. The absence of noise was foreign and slightly confusing until she noticed a very subtle wave of some music that seemed to be part of the air. It was to be experienced, but not exactly identifiable as something breaking the sanctity of the silence. She saw elevators opening and closing to move people throughout the building, but there were no sounds save the floating music which was more like breath inhaled. She let the music wash through her as she was drawn to a lone desk of shining metal. This building was far different, and more imposing, than the one where their initial applications were processed. There was no person at the desk but somehow, she knew that she would be received.

As she walked to the desk, a small monitor panel raised, displaying a message:

**"Please show your personal identification.
Thank you."**

She responded to the unspoken request by raising her
wrist to the monitor. The identification was little more than
a small QR code tattooed on the wrist. Everyone on the
planet had one, it was required for personal identification,
employment, health records, and just about everything that
could be loaded into the Nano-data receptors stored in the
small image. When she and James applied to transport to
Eros, all the medical and psychological test data had been
loaded into the QR. If for some reason, their applications
had been rejected, the volumes of data would be backed up
to the I.O.T.A.A. database and the QR redone with a
rejection code. A person would, however, be allowed to
reapply to a different planet that better suited their profile.
In some cases, I.O.T.A.A. would suggest an optional
transport, but she and James had only one desire. The laser
scan made a single pass across her QR followed by a new
message on the monitor:

> **"Mrs. Angela Drummond, please step to
> Elevator number 4 to your left in the wall
> behind this desk. Thank you and have a
> nice day."**

She did as the message instructed and moved to the 4th
door panel. Upon entering the elevator, she noticed there
were no buttons to push, but she had not received any
instructions on what floor to go to either. Then the monitor
on the wall lit up with a new message:

> **"Please provide your Identification to
> select your floor number."**

Again, she raised her wrist to be scanned. The monitor displayed:

"Thank you, Mrs. Drummond."

The doors silently closed, and the elevator must have been moving, but there was no sound or sense of vertical movement. The elevator stopped to pick up two more people, each scanning their QR's and being addressed by their names. One more stop and the monitor lit up:

"Mrs. Drummond, please exit and step to the monitor on your right."

Compliance again, but for some reason, she was pleased to be out of the strange elevator. Prepared to show her ID now, she stepped quickly to the monitor, her QR ready to be scanned. The monitor displayed:

"Thank You, Mrs. Drummond, your agent will be with you directly."

"Hmmm", she thought, *"no reference to what office or room to go to..."* Then she looked down the long hallway and it occurred to her that she could see no doors, doorways, doorknobs, or numbers on what seemed to be a solid blank wall. Suddenly, down the hall, she saw a brighter rectangular light on the wall and when she blinked at the unexpected change, she saw a woman walking in her direction.

The woman soundlessly approached Angie. The diminutive size of this woman reminded Angie of the images of meadow willows she'd seen in E-books. She had never been outside the confines of the endless concrete walls of business and apartment structures. The woman smiled a rather practiced looking smile and said nothing but gracefully put her hand out to indicate for Angie to lead the way to the white opening in the wall. As they walked to the 'doorway' Angie felt, not heard, the woman speak to her. The woman said, "Welcome to I.O.T.A.A., I will be your assistant as you prepare for your journey to Eros". Angie was pretty sure that the woman had made no sound to break the silence, yet she knew what the woman's message to her was. It didn't occur to Angie to look to see if the woman's lips had moved during the brief one-way conversation. She suspected that if she had tried to speak, her words would not have broken the silence of the building.

Stepping into the light in the wall Angie found herself in a very simple and sparsely furnished office where she was offered a very comfortable chair. The woman spoke again, this time introducing herself as Miss Seconds, Mrs. Drummond's transport coordinator. She had two small clear-screen tablets in front of her, one of which she handed to Angie. As Miss Seconds gracefully swiped through pages of the images and data loaded into the Angela Drummond file folder, Angie again realized that she 'felt' the introduction and didn't exactly hear it, so she mentally resolved to pay attention to the next time Miss Seconds 'spoke'.

As Miss Seconds asked Angie if she had a list of questions, Angie noticed that Miss Seconds' face was looking down at the tablet as the file pages were sliding swiftly across the clear screen. Once again, Angie was unable to see if Miss Seconds' mouth had actually moved.

"*Oh well,*" thought Angie, "*my mind is spinning and I'm probably imagining things*", so she began with her questions about the transport. She no longer noticed that Miss Seconds' mouth never changed from the graceful smile, or that the responses were more felt than heard. Much literature was instantly shared between the tablets as Miss Seconds spun through the volumes with the skill of a practiced magician. She quickly accessed E-brochures which she provided in answer to Angie's many questions.

Angie wanted to know why she was denied the ability to take personal items and clothing for the transport. She would have preferred to take pictures of her mother, her wedding ring, and small treasures to remind her of her relationships on Earth. Miss Seconds quickly shared an E-brochure that showed women wearing one-piece medical-style paper jumpsuits, no jewelry showing while pointing to the images. These images demonstrated that the transport process followed a thorough decontamination procedure to ensure the greatest safety of the residents of the host planet. Angie felt a little foolish about her question. "*Of course, it was important to the people of Eros to be protected, especially from any planet Earth bacteria,*", she thought, "*since Eros is a planet devoted to reproduction, children and families.*" The following E-brochures showed pictures of women on Eros wearing all manner of clothing, and most apparent – no uniforms. They were wearing colorful dresses and other apparel. More photos of couples and families and yes indeed the women were wearing wedding rings in the lovely colored E-brochures.

Miss Seconds reminded her that one regulated size box could be packed for transport to be received at a later date. A non-organic transport needed to be done from a different location in the United States and Mrs. Drummond would be in immunological quarantine for two months. Most often, the traveler's package, including the tablet and any photos from earth stored for future viewing, would arrive before the end of the quarantine. Miss Seconds scrolled to the chapter in the E-brochure that explained the reason for the separate transports and suggested that Angie might read this section if she required further explanation as to why there was a need for the two different types of transport.

Angie had forgotten the information about the arrival quarantine and felt compelled to inquire if the process was a strictly confined area or room. She again received a new E-brochure showing women in different comfortable-looking quarters containing furniture and a dining area set with platters of vivid colored fruits and vegetables.

Suddenly, Angie began to feel warm and calm as she asked for information about the planet, such as median temperature, types of recreation and job opportunities for women. The responses were tailor-made to match her volumes of application data. Of course, women were allowed to work if they chose to do so and virtually all businesses facilitated the working mothers by providing onsite childcare. The mother was always just a few minutes from any child incident that needed to be addressed. She said that working mothers were encouraged to participate in a limited number of childcare hours each month as part of their employment agreement.

Miss Seconds discussed the greater nutritional value of the produce on Eros, explaining that it was not uncommon for working mothers to sometimes choose to work more hours simply because they had more energy from the change in diet on Eros. Employers preferred a structured number of working hours to ensure that the marital needs were satisfied in addition to the quality family time needed to raise the children. No women were required to work, it was an option. Eros's policies were founded on the belief that the family unit was the highest priority in its culture.

Information was shared to her tablet that explained how the lower gravity would take some time to adjust to. A person felt lighter and needed to learn to walk a little slower and softer on Eros while the internal organs adjusted to the reduced strain. There was also information about the change of atmosphere causing increased libido, which would seem foreign initially, but easily adapted to.

She wanted to know if she would be able to reconnect with her husband while in quarantine and was told it could not be physical, but video conferencing was encouraged. In essence, it was video foreplay to encourage spouses to prepare for their exciting reunion. She was told that most travelers inseminate within the first two weeks of reuniting with their respective spouses. This was a very exciting prospect for Angie!

Once Angie could think of no more questions, Miss Seconds shared the legal documents for Angie's signatures. There were payment completion agreement signatures, the release of assets to I.O.T.A.A., and liability disclaimers. Then there were insurance beneficiary documents that required I.O.T.A.A. be the primary beneficiary until the quarantine period was completed. This was a formality really to protect the agency from a compromise of their investment capital in the unlikely event of a complication. Once a traveler arrived at their destination and completed their quarantine period, they would be allowed to change the designation and install the spouse as the primary beneficiary.

Finally, with all documents signed and questions asked and answered, Miss Seconds sent the link which included Angie's flight authorization to the transport site one week from tomorrow. As Miss Seconds rose to escort Angie to the elevators, the wall appeared to open, the unusual doorway again distracted her from noticing that Miss Seconds' mouth did not change from the smile as she said, "Mrs. Drummond, your week of work has just begun, it is time to plan to close your life on planet Earth as you prepare to start your new life."

Fortunately, she had enough presence of mind when she left the building to take some pictures with the little tablet, which she intended to share the following day at work. The images she had taken of the wall of mirrors covered with what looked like thousands of people would be very entertaining to her fellow apartment dwellers who had never been to the big city center of Atlanta.

Following three transport transfers back to her apartment Angie realized that most of her day had slipped away. The entire morning had been surreal. Her apartment friends had organized a pseudo surprise party for her. There were dozens of neighboring apartment dwellers awkwardly jammed into the tiny apartment. She was thankful to the landlord for allowing this rare community get-together. There was a variety of finger foods waiting and many more good wishes. Fortunately, there were only a few baby shower-type gifts that would need to be refunded. The well-wishers were unaware that nothing of that nature would be allowed to be transported, but she didn't feel like explaining those details. Instead, she showed the E-brochure links on the small clear tablet that had been provided by Miss Seconds at the earlier meeting.

The gathering lasted late into the night as her friends poured over the E-brochures on the tablet with the beautiful photos of Eros and its lush green gardens and cropland covered with brilliantly colored fruits and vegetables. There were no images of concrete or apartment buildings. This envious group just couldn't bear to leave without seeing every photo and E-brochure that seemed like a stream of dreams that could only be imagined before this day.

She had so much to do with only six days remaining. The morning following the apartment gathering arrived much too soon for her. She was pretty sure that the remaining workdays would be the least productive in her career. Then came the epiphany! It didn't matter if she worked or not. She wouldn't be taking any work credits with her, and she had plenty of food in the apartment for the remaining days. She might as well just give her resignation and get about the business of preparing for the new 'Eros-life' as she'd decided to dub the future. "*As a matter of fact,*" thought Angie, "*I may as well E-comm my resignation right now and begin to plan my departure.*"

Of course, the company had known about her planned departure and was prepared with a list of suitable candidates to interview for her position. Her E-comm was merely a formality for them to open the process of replacing her. It was a win-win from the perspective of the company. They would be able to replace her with a younger person who could be hired for fewer wage credits. Elective departures were, for the most part, financially beneficial to businesses as there was never a shortage of young, hungry resources from which to choose.

She would need to find new owners for all non-attached living quarter items. That would be easy as she would only need to launch a small E-comm out that these items would be available for immediate removal on the designated date. The bed was part of the wall, and the few small chairs were easily portable from the tiny apartment. People didn't really 'cook' on Earth now, so the kitchen was little more than an eating bar. Normally they ate the government-provided Food Ration Packets that satisfied nutritional requirements but discouraged over-eating due to their lack of taste. In the E-brochures within her new best friend the Eros-Tablet, there were many pictures of vivid colored foods inviting the viewer to 'just take a big bite!' The E-brochures were scattered throughout with photo images of smiling parents and multiple shining face children in multicolored clothing. The fantasies of her life were there in living color, and she knew soon she would be enjoying that life.

Her employment credits were now frozen due to her signed I.O.T.A.A. contract, but she had uniforms and some stockpiled Food Ration Packets to trade for anything she might yet need. And then... A knock on the door interrupted her reverie. She quickly opened the door to receive the approved transport box from the delivery service. The container was 203mm x 280mm x 101mm deep. Inside were two small compartments, snapping lids were presumably intended to protect something such as her wedding band from getting loose in whatever else she put in the non-compartmentalized section. One of the two snapping compartments seemed to have shielded walls that contained a memory stick onto which she would load her photos "*Well this transport container put a new spin on traveling light*", she thought. But she placed her ring into one of the snap-locking sections and began to go through her photos to see which ones would be transferred to the memory stick and returned to the shielded compartment. The selection and transfer of her personal document and image files took the remainder of her day as she ruminated over each picture and made notations about each. She added the many years of E-diaries that she'd written sharing her frustration at being unable to conceive even as they had finally been authorized to do so. The following half-day finished the memory stick project. As she inserted the stick into the shielded compartment, she looked at the space remaining in the transport box and thought about what she should add to that small but vacuous looking area.

She went to the tiny closet that housed her uniforms and clothing garments. As she opened the drawer that housed her undergarments and socks, she retrieved from the rear a small baby rattle made of yellow chewable vinyl. This was the most precious item, and she would have it waiting for her when she finished her quarantine. As she snapped the transport box closed, it occurred to her that she had no memory of her husband filling a transport container or his wedding ring. It was just a year ago, but why she had no memories of this process when he was preparing to depart for Eros was a mystery to her.

The closet garments were now neatly stacked and placed in a small reusable box for distribution to the needy. "*Well,*" she thought, "*there is one less thing to do.*" Hair and hygiene items were dispensed through the shower with the push of a button, so there were no toiletries to be disposed of. She had expected that the remaining days would be packed with things to do, but here she found herself with nothing undone or planned for. As she looked at the calendar on her watch, she was surprised to realize that she had lost track of a couple of days of her life in the 'sorting' process, but that was ok. She would love to just go to sleep and wake up on the departure day if that had been possible.

She E-comm'd an apartment friend that she knew was financially comfortable. Angie asked if they could go out on Zimm's credits, in exchange for some pantry or clothing items that were no longer needed. Zimm was happy to have a night out with her and of course, she had credits for their celebration. The evening with Zimm went great. They went to clubs that single women frequented to seek out attractive single men. Zimm was a flirt, but she had no interest in husband-hunting. She had opted to be sterilized in her early teens knowing that she'd rather enjoy the pleasures of sex without the accidental pregnancies which would have meant forced abortions. Nope, for Zimm it was all about enjoying the small free things in life without consequences. "OH", she told Angie, "I didn't mean small things when it came to personal pleasure!" They had laughed at the double meaning until they arrived at the club district.

Street noise was a normal part of life, but the noise of a club was something entirely unknown to Angie. The music and movement were felt throughout the body more than the sound of the chaos. They danced and drank as the men swarmed the single women like steel filings to a magnet. The drinking and chaos put Angie in a world of color and sensation that was foreign to her, but she allowed it to carry her through the evening. Zimm seemed to disappear at some point, probably off in another area enjoying the 'not-small' pleasures to which they had laughed about on the ride to the district. So many men were advancing, dancing, and bringing more drinks, all obvious in their sexual interest in occupying her time.

Perhaps there had been drugs introduced into the many trays of drinks that appeared without her noticing them being ordered. Somehow the fantasy and chaos became the reality and she found herself engaging in sex with one of the men who had been persistent in his advances. He was younger than James but adept at reminding her of what she had been missing for the last year of her husband's absence. She hadn't asked if he was sterile, she was only thinking with her body now. She had lost track of time and the world around her until Zimm tapped her foot and said, "Time to go now, Miss Horny Hanna". Angie had no memory of the trip home and when she finally woke, she discovered that she was now only a day away from her transport.

After a steaming shower and review of the many 'sexual activity marks' on her body, she decided it best to sit and write a communique to James. Not a confession of indiscretion, but just a message to end her life on Earth as he'd done a year before. She hoped that he had not been 'weak' as she had been the previous night when she and Zimm had gone out, but if he had, she was sure she would find a way to forgive him.

My Darling James,

Tomorrow is the day I will finally fly to the CA Territories for my teleport to Eros. They tell me that I will be in quarantine for two months but that we will be able to video conference as much as we want, and I look forward very much to hearing the many things you have been doing since you were released from your quarantine. None of the E-comms from you state if you are working there, but I can only assume that you have been hard at work on the beautiful planet. I can hardly wait to share the new world with you as we begin creating a family.

They tell me that my communique will arrive after me, but I just felt that I should send one last message from Earth to you, my darling.

Much love, Angie

She took a sleeping pill, there was no way she would be able to sleep this final night in her apartment without it. In the morning after her shower, the people came to pick up the remainders of her personal effects as the apartment was emptied to prepare for new paint and new residents. The transport arrived and Angie with her small transport box left for the last time. There was a two-hour ride to the airport where she was escorted to an I.O.T.A.A. terminal to board the flight to the GaliPort location in the CA Territories. Her transport container was collected at the check-in counter, where it was tagged after confirming her identity and transport codes from the QR code on her wrist. She was then escorted by a demure willowy lady wearing a deep ocean blue I.O.T.A.A. uniform. The escort led her with gentle movements of the hands, never speaking, only wearing a fixed smile.

The aerial transport was small but comfortable with seating for thirty people. She was seated next to a handsome executive-looking businessman. After take-off, she found her voice and asked him what planet his destination was. He said his name was David Arthur and he was going to Mercari – the commerce planet. He was a broker involved in the exportation of certain rare earth minerals known to exist in abundance on the planet named TerreOra. It had a small population insufficient to extract that and other metals which were so precious to Earth. He then politely inquired about Angie's destination. They spent the next hours discussing their reasons for the escape to the alternate planets and Angie was much calmer from chatting with such an intelligent person as this gentleman who helped the time pass more quickly. She had never been on an aerial transport before or even out of the city, so his experience and manner were good fortunes for Angie. He spent time sharing the history of the teleportation process as she had seemed to be woefully uninformed about the program.

In the United States, there were two intergalactic teleportation facilities, both in the CA Territories. The GaliPort was closer to the desert area inland where the state of Nevada used to be. The GaliWorm was near the Pacific coast because of the proximity to international transportation systems for moving commodities arriving from the outer galactic planets. The GaliWorm locations were easily accessible to ocean shipping, rail, and other transport options for continental as well as intercontinental distribution. They were a mecca of international commerce and warehousing with millions of job opportunities to keep the distribution centers moving products all year long.

The two methods of intergalactic transportation were quite different. The first to be developed was the GaliWorm and was the method of transporting craft through wormholes in space to arrive at the various planets able to sustain life. Once the craft and method were tested for reliability, they were able to determine that the average earth's physical time from departure to the habitable planets ranged from three to six weeks. This method of transportation was dubbed GaliWorm for its use of wormholes for connecting two locations in the Universe. A GaliWorm trip could be a bumpy ride because the wormholes tended to be tumultuous. The main use of the 'worm' was for the transport of non-organic materials such as building materials, minerals, and equipment which needed to be protected from the electro-magnetic impacts such travel could have on sensitive devices. It was safer to transport the controls and electronics for equipment in separate shielded containers for assembly at the destination planets. I.O.T.A.A. developed a line of transport crafts that would be more organic friendly but even these were at the mercy of the six weeks of in-stasis hibernation for human organic transport and considered to be 'burdensome' and physically risky to organics.

Fortunately, the alien and human scientists were able to collaborate to develop the teleportation device which allowed the folding of the time/space continuum. This precipitated the launch of the current human GaliPort systems that provided the molecular transport of organic material without the need for homeostasis, specialty transport devices, or wormhole trauma. The amount of time it took to transport a human through a GaliPort was only minutes, while physiological lapse was from three to six weeks. For example, if a plant sprout that normally would take twelve weeks to mature is sent through GaliPort, it arrives minutes after departure. The plant would be equal to a six-week-old plant. Mortal teleportation similarly aged the traveler somewhat, but without the trauma or homeostasis risks involved with a GaliWorm transport.

Once David had given her the history lesson of the teleportation systems, he suggested that Angie might enjoy wearing the headphones on the remainder of the trip to the CA Territories. She agreed to try them and found the pleasant music that she remembered from just a week ago – the soft whispering music that seems to become part of a person's breathing rather than just audible sounds. She quickly slipped into a gentle cradle of sleep where she dreamed the image of her yellow rattle floating in and out of her view as the gentle music ebbed and flowed.

David Arthur knew much about what her future held on Eros, but she wasn't the first Eros-bound woman he'd sat beside on the way to CA Territories. Angie didn't know that the seating had been arranged in advance to ensure that she would be insulated from any other person designated for Eros. A single small detail like a chance communication could be the thing that would bring down the house of cards. I.O.T.A.A. had too many galactic irons in the fire to leave things to chance. In the past, there had been enough accidents and errors to jeopardize the program. They knew there would be incidents again, but they were doing their best to remove as many trip wires as possible.

The decontamination process on Earth would take both Angie and David about three hours before they would be moved in sterile isolation transport vehicles to the actual GaliPort. Their destinations would be pre-programmed into their QRs before the decontamination processing. Once they were individually escorted into the sterile GaliPort room, the door would close and they would, in seconds, arrive at their programmed destinations. The GaliPort room only transported one person at a time. The QR destination program would, in theory, ensure that multiple people could travel from the same room, but genetic mixing was a 'risk' that I.O.T.A.A. would not currently consider taking. They did not like to leave things to chance.

Angie slept her peaceful musical sleep until David touched her arm to tell her they were about to arrive at GaliPort and perhaps she would like to see it from the air before they landed. She immediately sat up and looked out the window to see the huge expanse of desert broken by many straight roads leading to the hub which was a pyramid-looking building and must surely be the GaliPort. The area around the pyramid was as fortified as any military base she'd seen images of but had a surprisingly small amount of vehicle parking areas between the pyramid and the landing pad, to which they were descending. Angie had never, in real life, seen so much open space as what surrounded this complex and knew she would have a difficult time recording in her diary the images and emotions of the spectacular scene before her.

Departure was quick and silent. Angie hadn't noticed that there were so many people on the flight. But it was too late to try to connect with them as they were escorted to waiting transports which seemed to only hold two people plus the driver. David had done this before, so he continued in his silent amusement as he watched Angie's head swivel trying to memorize each wonderful vision before her. She seemed like a nice lady, and it was unfortunate for her that she'd chosen Eros. There were no return transports from Eros, and he had heard stories of life there. In his mind, he hummed the ancient tune, *'Welcome to the Hotel California....You can check out any time you like but you can nevvver leave...'*

When her escort received her, she raised her wrist to display her QR. *"This is getting to be a habit,"* Angie thought as she followed the person in the GaliPort badged jumpsuit to the transport vehicle. There were two seats in the rear, divided by a thick clear shield but thankfully, the music floated into her senses with each breath. The trip from the landing pad to the decontamination building was short, leaving little time to get panicked. There were two escorts at the Decontamination building, separately taking care of their traveler charges, again verifying the QR and quickly moving into the Decom building. Once inside the small room, she encountered a monitor to scan her QR again before receiving the instructions:

> **"Please remove all articles of clothing, Mrs. Angela Drummond. There is a container on your left to deposit all items. When you are finished, please step through the airlock to your right where you will begin your decontamination process. Thank you, Mrs. Drummond."**

The walls of the room were shiny metal, and one wall was mirrored, apparently for her to make sure she had taken everything off. She did as had been requested and in the mirror noticed again the marks on her body from her evening out with Zimm -- her indiscretion night. She sighed with relief at the knowledge that the marks would be gone before she completed her quarantine period on Eros. She then stepped into the airlock leading to the first decontamination shower. Like any other shower, it involved her washing her hair and body with a shower wand producing antiseptic smelling suds. The monitor in this room was larger and it prompted her to pay more attention to certain parts of her body. It only took one prompt for her to realize that she was being observed, so she was more meticulous after the warning.

Subsequent decontamination rooms involved more invasive cleaning techniques making her feel uncomfortable as the processes involved mechanical attendance to certain orifices. She just kept her focus on the prize, this violation process would have to be done again on Eros, but after that, she would be able to start a family with her beloved James.

The process did indeed take about two hours but in the end, she was the cleanest she'd ever been in her entire life as she awaited the escort to dress her. Hair covering, then mask followed by gloves, jumpsuit, and foot booties. The escort was wearing an identical set of garbs, except that Angie's was stenciled with her QR on the chest of the jumpsuit. She started to ask the escort a question but was met with a finger to the lips to indicate that no verbal communication was allowed now. The escort pointed to the monitor. It displayed:

> **"Mrs. Drummond, you have been decontaminated, please refrain from any verbal communication, you will be transported in six minutes. Thank you and have a nice trip to Eros."**

"*SIX MINUTES???*", thought Angie. "*I don't believe it !!!*" The escort walked her through another corridor where they entered a new larger chamber. The escort then exited leaving her alone in the middle of the room. There was a large monitor on the wall. It was counting down.

T minus 5...4...3...2...1

At T minus 2, Angie took a deep breath, she was expecting some loud noise or explosive pressure, but there was nothing...

She looked at the monitor:

> **"Welcome to Eros, Mrs. Drummond, We hope you had a timeless trip, your escort will join you directly."**

She collapsed onto the floor before the escort entered. There was a slightly audible alarm, then the monitor showed:

> **"Please rise, Mrs. Drummond, your faint is not uncommon. You must be decontaminated now. Please depart the landing area with your escort immediately. If you are unable to rise, you will be assisted. Thank you."**

She got up from the soft floor and followed the escort to begin the decontamination process again. This process was similar and followed by several hours of temperature and blood tests while she was in a comfortable hospital-looking bed. She noticed in the decontamination shower, that her bruises were completely gone now, but that her breasts were very tender and wondered if she had injured herself when she fainted in the teleport arrival room. But the floor had been soft, like foam and she thought she might ask a doctor about that.

The monitor on the wall lit up and displayed:

"Mrs. Drummond your tests have been completed and you will be escorted to your quarantine location. Do you have any questions that Medical can respond to?"

"Well," said Angie, "I was wondering if I somehow sustained an injury in the transport."

The monitor responded:

"Medical shows no indication of injury to Mrs. Drummond."

"Oh, my breasts are very tender and feeling rather swollen, I know that I fell in the transport room when I arrived. I thought perhaps I was injured in some way."

After a brief delay, the monitor engaged again:

"That is perfectly normal for a six-week pregnancy Mrs. Drummond, the tenderness will subside."

"OH NO", said Angie, "you must be mistaken, I'm not pregnant!! I haven't been with my husband for nearly a year!!"

Another brief delay and then:

"Your transport process is equal to 6 weeks of human time Mrs. Drummond, there is no doubt about your pregnancy status, your insemination would have been approximately three to four Earth days ago. Your gestation period on earth would be approximately 25.4 Earth weeks. The nutritional change on Eros will accelerate the gestation process by

approximately 40 percent so the Eros delivery time will be expected to be approximately 10.17 weeks. Congratulations Mrs. Drummond."

Angie fainted.

CERES

Ceres is a planet that is orbiting two suns equidistant from each other. This unique location provides 24-hour sunlight around the planet. The native population species of the planet exists primarily underground.

The constant surface ultraviolet exposure was the cause of the near extinction of the population until they moved underground. The result of subterranean living on Ceres was limitless agricultural opportunities for the Earth imported scientific farmers as there was little need to waste surface space for habitation or industry. Their knowledge about the processes of crop rotation and fertilization to promote continuing healthy soil was exactly what Ceres needed. The ancient above-ground buildings were replaced by parking centers and paved grid roads for the movement of farming equipment that would be stored in new storage buildings, leaving a nearly endless surface of lush plant life. Droids were now used for monitoring crops. Each equipment pad held one large building which contained a transport elevator that brought the small quantities of underground dwellers to the surface to work the fields or maintain the equipment, activities not performed by the droids. Of course, there was the GaliPort pyramid and the GaliWorm hub which transported the people and produce of Ceres to other planets. Aside from these organized infrastructures, the planet seemed to be endlessly green.

There had been initial challenges in the pollination of the plants as the planet had no natural means for this process. A collaboration with robotics scientists and farmers resulted in a method of aerial 'vacuum' and redistribution which provided robust pollination programs. Some entomologists on planet Earth worked with bees in their laboratories to genetically engineer a species that was adaptable to the Ceres ultraviolence. Simultaneously, mechanical engineers worked to devise organic transport containers which would allow the transport of the newly engineered bees which previously couldn't survive the normal GaliWorm transport process.

* * *

Ahlyeksyey Turgenev, known to all as Alexi, was a commodities broker born in Moscow. He was sitting at one of the many sidewalk cafés waiting for his lady friend, Antonia Ivanov. He smiled as she walked up. She was, as always, beautiful with her chestnut-colored hair swirling in the summer wind. He would love to marry her, but he knew the answer would be no. She was still married to the father of her daughter Marta, even though she had no idea where the foolish man had gone when he departed years ago. She couldn't be divorced from someone who could not be located.

She greeted him with a smile brighter than the summer sun — he was hopelessly in love with her. Perhaps today his proposal would be accepted. "My precious Antonia, sweeter than the tea I have waiting for you, I have missed you these many weeks as I traveled the universe for you, no for us, my sweet!"

"Oh Lexi, tell me about your travels, I see your skin is darkened from your time on the other planet! Tell me the tales that have brought the smile to your face and the bloom to your skin color."

"I bring you happy news and another proposal, my dear. Just yesterday I spent the day with the ministry of commerce finalizing my submissions, and I have the approval to begin the new enterprise on the planet Ceres! I've been granted the position of Ambassador of Commerce to the planet. There I will be in charge of the purchase and shipment of agricultural products from this lovely productive planet to export and feed the families of Russia!"

Her smile faded as though a cloud passed across the sun. "Does this mean...that you will live there on Ceres?"

"My darling Antonia, I could not live any place in the universe that would deny me the beauty of your smile or the touch of your skin. I have received approval for you to come with me, you and Marta also! We will no longer suffer the cold winters or food lines, my sweet. My proposal to you is to share your life with me until my contacts in Russia find that fool that would leave you. He will be found, and you will be free to say yes when I beg for your hand in marriage."

"Yes, Yes, Yes, I will of course go with you. What will Marta do there? She is a young woman, with a simple job here but it gives her some freedom from the overbearing mother."

"She will be able to work on Ceres. The 'cities' of Ceres are underground but have all the amenities of life on the surface here. I will ensure that my contract includes that she is provided the opportunity for a career suited to her talents and a personal residence so that she may have the freedom of a young woman while the mother is free to enjoy the passions of her future husband. Once you have gotten her approval to make the move, I will make the arrangements for us to transport to St. Petersburg and the GaliPort there. You must talk with her and take the time to say goodbye to your friends here on Earth. I don't believe that, once we have moved there, we would want to return to Russia. Please join me tonight so that I might remember your body again before I return to Ceres. I will have to return in three days where I will secure a perfect location for us in the city on Ceres, I will return so that we might transport together for the final move."

As a Russian exporter, Alexi had been negotiating with David Arthur for several years trying to convince Arthur to continue exporting Russian grain products to the United States rather than from other planets. But they both knew that the Russian grain production was no longer sufficient to feed the needs of a burgeoning global population. It made more sense to import the materials from another, more productive planet. They were well acquainted with one another and held mutual respect, despite their differences in the best prices for their respective exports. Now, with Alexi's ambassadorship on Ceres secured, and the products under his control, grain import and export could continue with greater success for the Earth and other planets.

Two weeks later, Alexi, Antonia, and Marta were transported to the agricultural planet of Ceres. Living underground proved to be a pleasant change from the unpredictable weather of Russian seasons. The city had controlled lighting to simulate day and night times while temperatures were constant and comfortable for homo sapiens as well as other lifeforms. In the case of most non-humans, some required adjustments in their living accommodations, and special outerwear was worn to adjust their personal comfort for the time spent in the 'city streets'. The residents of Ceres were equipped with small translator devices that provided ease of communication between the various intergalactic residents. Marta quickly assimilated and even made a small circle of friends including non-Earth peers.

Her mother Antonia, after their initial shopping trips, had been remote as the amount of time she spent with Alexi was significant. This was fine with Marta, an independent young woman, who enjoyed the freedom and distance break from her mother. She was disappointed however to find that Ceres was a 'dry planet' in that there was no alcohol to be found. This was unthinkable for Marta coming from a country where the drinking of copious amounts of vodka was a part of life.

Marta had 'alien friends' one named TRKNIS. She dubbed this friend Trish which was more easily pronounced. Trish had a father involved in the grape harvesting while another Earth friend from the USA named Derik worked the fields of potatoes. Those two ingredients were most of what Marta needed to begin her enterprise. She asked her mother to get Alexi to import pallets of sugar and yeast. Antonia asked why she would need such volumes of these items but accepted her daughter's explanation that these items were needed to start a bakery shop. Indeed, the trio of young people opened a storefront filled with baked goods, but the larger rear portion of the structure housed vats of fermenting grapes and potatoes for the manufacture of wine and vodka. As the months continued, the young people of Ceres quickly found backdoor access to the alcohols produced in Marta's cottage business which was thriving. The credits in her profit margin were far more than her future stepfather's ambassadorship provided.

Six months into Marta's bakery enterprise, she informed Alexi and Antonia that she needed a small beekeeping business to provide local honey for her bakery shelves to sell with her loaves of bread. But of course, they were delighted to assist her in her fledgling business. They had no idea that the honey was being turned primarily into honey vodka.

Ceres had previously been a 'dry country' but in a year, the young persons of the small underground city began to suffer acute alcoholism while the controlling entities continued to be stymied over the 'illness' which swept through the youth population. The second year brought the expansion of Marta's bootleg alcohol enterprise to other underground cities including her newest product Ceres Honey Vodka.

Eventually, the Ceres Honey Vodka came to the attention of Alexi and though he didn't know it was a product manufactured by his stepdaughter, he enjoyed the vodka very much and decided to begin exporting it to Russia. The grains shipped from Ceres went to Mother Russia, Alexi did not benefit from the grain products because he was paid to be an ambassador and broker. The vodka enterprise was a financial nest egg that Russia was unable to benefit from or take away. He rather enjoyed becoming a capitalist.

His export relationship with David Arthur was yet another opportunity for Alexi and his family. Exporting the vodka from Ceres bypassed the distillation taxes imposed on alcohol produced on Earth.

* * *

Ceres began to see a rather alarming number of deaths in the non-human population. After several hundreds of deaths, the physicians discovered that the cause was not as previously diagnosed as overindulgence in alcohol, but that the cold-blooded lifeforms did not have a liver organ similar to a human. The lack of a liver to filter the alcohol out of the system led to death from the accumulation of the poison. It was the repeated consumption by the lifeforms that was the cause as the toxic alcohol simply never leaving their systems.

Once the cause of the deaths was identified, Marta and

her partners quickly discontinued the selling of the alcohol until her sales outlets were advised to prohibit the sale to non-human buyers. Fortunately for Marta, her business was still anonymous during this temporary prohibition. She and her business partners quickly began to manufacture non-alcoholic varieties of the products to safely increase her sales. Her name for the non-alcoholic honey vodka was Noney Honey which was a great hit throughout the non-human and non-drinking population.

The small quantities of Ceres Honey Vodka that Alexi had been exporting to Russia were black market, with a low-profit margin. During a family dinner, he mentioned this vodka enterprise and that he'd like to find the owner to negotiate an export deal. Finally, Marta needed to reveal to Alexi and her mother that the wine and vodkas were her products. Rather than the expected fury, her news was met with great joy and the proposal to expand the business enterprise to a commercial manufacturing opportunity, which he would be proposing to his export broker and friend on Mercari, David Arthur.

Throughout the evening the family planned the logistics of the future expansion to convert to a commercial enterprise on the surface. Alexi would have a dome built to house the bee farm, designed to protect the bees from the 24-hour UV bombardment. The lighting in the dome would be controlled to simulate the day/night environment in which the bees would thrive. He would ask David to locate an apiculturist – to be hired to live on the planet and manage the bees' productivity.

I.O.T.A.A.

MERCARI

Being from the southeastern part of the United States, David Arthur had a taste for the summer gold 'Mint Julep'. Although Mercari had some alcohol, bourbon was not on the list of very expensive imported spirits. When he heard from the club bartender about new alcohol production on the planet of Ceres, he was pleased to know that it would be transported without going through the Earth taxation process and he was delighted to try some of Ceres's products.

He found the wine too sweet for his taste, but the Honey Vodka reminded him of Southern Comfort. He tried several mixtures and settled on a combination of the Honey Vodka with a splash of tonic and twists of lemon and lime to temper the sweetness. He dubbed his potable 'Cerestini' which quickly became the most popular drink at many of the clubs on Mercari.

It didn't take long to develop a universal market for the bottles of the pre-mixed Cerestini, 'Just shake and garnish', cocktail. The product wasn't sold in U.S. Earth markets, he refused to pay the huge distillation taxes that the U.S. Earth wanted to impose. After reaching out to collaborate with his old friend from Russia, he agreed to market the Ceres, wine, and vodka products with his Cerestini. It was logical to have his product manufactured there on Ceres using the currently lucrative distillation process managed there by Alexi Turgenev and stepdaughter Marta Ivanov. Alexi, Antonia, and Marta now enjoyed the capitalist lifestyle and their relationship with the very knowledgeable American, Mr. Arthur.

His reason for working on Mercari was the ability to broker items from many planets to Earth and other planets based on their needs. He was the 'Supply Guy' who could get what you needed if the price was right. The planet TerreOra was rich with noble and non-noble metals, ores, and rare earth minerals. The mining of rare earth minerals was very lucrative because it was a by-product of the extraction of other products on TerreOra. Rare earth minerals were used in virtually all electronic devices on Earth, which in the universal plan was pretty backward in technology, but at this time, was still in great demand on Earth. The previous main source of the rare earth minerals happened to be Russia, but its mines were being depleted. Earthlings had not evolved to ESP communication; thus, they were dependent upon communication devices. Supply and demand, of course, demanded higher prices, so it made sense for him to connect with the bountiful TerreOra to replace the mineral and ore competition on Earth.

He also discovered in his research that the non-human life forms of TerreOra were diminishing as working the mines seemed to cause sterility in both men and women. He quickly devised an ad hoc Jobs Agency to bring in more experienced and physically hardy mine workers. He could offer higher wages and housing benefits for those who had wives who tested positive for fertility capability. TerraOra, his 'gravy boat' as he began referring to it, would have some breeding stock born and raised to be miners.

While speaking with a Mercari club member, the slightly

intoxicated David related his ideas about TerraOra. "From what I've found in my research, there has been a sort of compound established to raise children until they are old enough to become miners or breeders."

The friend asked, "So what happens when the women are beyond procreation age, Dave? What if they could be used for entertainment purposes?"

"I frankly think the miners are too tired at night for extramarital stuff. But the miners still gotta eat and with the planet covered in mines, there won't be much in the way of food production." continued Dave. "But thanks for the question, I guess I will need to make sure I import several butchers also."

The comment was met with great laughter by both, but David knew his response wasn't said in jest. And with that, he excused himself to return to his office area in the posh resort to make a list of to-do items for his multi-faceted enterprises which would continue to be orchestrated from this lovely planet.

* * *

David Arthur had arrived on Mercari approximately twenty minutes after Angie Drummond had arrived on Eros. There was only a one-week-long quarantine on Mercari. Those Eros travelers needed more time to be indoctrinated into a new culture of slavery, if the stories he'd heard were true. But breeding slaves and trafficking were not going to be limited to Eros. He was going to need to employ a similar process for the miners of TerreOra.

Mercari was a beautiful vacation type of planet that appealed to educated and wealthy businesspeople. There were beaches, fine dining, arts, golf, gentlemen's clubs, and endless entertainment. He spent more time here than on Earth now because his brokerage companies were hugely successful and run by competent people in his absence. The quarantine period was spent in the company of professional female entertainment, which meant only that he had the freedom to exercise his desired level of baser or taboo behaviors without the possibility of offending the more gentile cultural norms of the planet.

He had a wife, well actually he had a few in different places, but they were trophy wives. They each knew their place and the consequences of letting themselves go. There was one, Breanna, who might earn herself a trip to Eros if she didn't shape up. He had plenty of connections in I.O.T.A.A. so getting a program change loaded into her QR to route her mouthy ass off to Eros would be easy to do. Or as he thought about it more, being sexually used or abused might be a reward for her rather than a punishment. Hephaestus would be a better location, as she could be hunted there like an animal. He hadn't heard much about the Vulcan planet other than the organized hunts that were booked well in advance of a traveler's arrival. He mused over the image of her trying to market her body to save herself from being murdered. "*Yes,*" he thought to himself, "*Hephaestus is just the trip for her. She will transport into the Prey bay, where she'll be held captive until it's time for a hunt.*"

Once Breanna was disposed of, he'd book a transport to Aphrodite where he would find a replacement for her, perhaps a more compliant female. Beauty was a good thing, but not if they wouldn't stay in line.

He went to get his tablet and prepared an E-comm for her.

Sweet Breanna, the weather here is amazing right now and I think because we were having difficulties the past few weeks, perhaps we could pull things back together here during a brief vacation. I promise I will not be working; it will just be you and me and the good things this planet has to offer.

I will have I.O.T.A.A. prepare a travel update to load to your QR. It will be ready and waiting by the time you get this message. Just log into your credit account and scan your QR, it will upload the travel date and send you a message of your departure date and time. You won't need to take any personal items. I will get you anything you need here on Mercari. Wishing I could be with you in decontamination if you get my meaning…

As always, David

His next message was to a contact at I.O.T.A.A.:

WIFE BREANNA – QR TO HEPHAESTUS – PREY BIN. Will await the sad news of her demise. I owe you one.

David

* * *

Just days later Breanna was preparing to join David. Monitor:

T minus 5…4…3…2…1

A moment later:

> **"Welcome to Hephaestus Mrs. Arthur. Please exit the doorway on your left. You will be escorted to your cell."**

"WHAT??? HEPHAESTUS??? CELL??" She was screaming at the monitor now. "You've made a mistake, I do not hunt, I was designated to transport to Mercari. WHAT THE HELL DO YOU MEAN CELL??? REPROGRAM ME AND SEND ME TO MERCARI IMMEDIATELY!!"

The monitor displayed:

> "We are sorry for your confusion Mrs. Arthur. Please exit through the door to your left."

"I AM NOT CONFUSED; you have made a mistake. This is insane, my husband is David Arthur, he is waiting for me on Mercari."

On the monitor:

> "We are sorry Mrs. Arthur, there is no mistake, please exit to the door to your left."

"Some alien f...king heads are gonna roll when he finds out about your mistake – I need a tablet – I need to contact him immediately and EVERY F...KING MINUTE I AM ON THIS PLANET IS GONNA COST SOME BUG EATING COLD BLOODED TUNNEL DWELLING SHIT ROLLING ALIEN...." And from the monitor display:

> "Mrs. Arthur, please step to the doorway on your left. Other travelers are awaiting reconstruction. If you do not comply, it will regrettably become necessary to have security restrain you before moving you to quarters."

Apparently, she was restrained as she now found herself seated in a chair in what appeared to be a common room. On her wrists were some metal cuffs that must be magnetic because she was unable to raise her arms. Her paper transport jumpsuit had been replaced with a sturdy camo uniform consisting of heavy fabric pants and a jacket.

There were three men in the room wearing similar attire. One was sitting in front of her looking at her face.

"Welcome to Wacky World. You've been out about forty minutes, you musta put up a hellova fight, Queen Arthur. My name is Cameron Wells, from Earth. Manchester in the UK. You can call me Ace if you want. That one over there I'm not sure about, but I'm calling him King, you Queen, and that skinny one near the corner crying, I'm calling him Joker. He won't last an hour in the hunt. I have no idea where those two came from or how tough they are, but they have never been Prey before. They're like you, sort of hunt virgins." He smiled.

Whatever they had zapped her with sure took some of the pack out of her punch. "Look," she said, "I'm here by mistake Ace. I was supposed to be transported to Mercari for vacation time with my husband. As soon as they figure it out, that they made a mistake, I'll be gone. I don't hunt. I never even touched a weapon. It was a total mistake to send me to a hunting planet, but I wish you well when you go shooting or whatever it is you do on the hunt. And can you please explain to me why I'm in restraints?"

Ace wanted to laugh out loud, but clearly, Queen Arthur hadn't figured out yet that, pretty as she was, she wasn't here to hunt but rather to be 'hunted'. It was a good bet that her presence in the Prey-Bay was not a mistake. But if he was to help her survive the hunt, he was going to have to make her understand her current position.

"Okay, Queen, I'm going to elucidate your current position, but you must promise to not start screaming and carrying on because that will just get you zapped again, and we don't have a lot of time to prepare for what is coming. So, you need to say, 'OK Ace' and keep your mouth shut".

"Ok Ace."

'You know that Hephaestus is a hunt planet, but I don't think you know what is hunted here. So, I must tell you why I'm here then maybe you will begin to understand things better. I was a businessman in the UK. My business partner had a way of doing things that weren't quite ethical or legal. When I discovered and threatened to expose her for what she'd been doing, she offered a hunting trip as contrition, with a promise to stop the illegal practices. She booked the trip for us, and I, like you, ended up in the Prey-Bay, not the Hunter Hotel transport. My partner had set me up to be a prey victim, to be killed with the knowledge I had of her crimes. The prey on this planet are two-legged animals, men and women of different species, but I don't know who organizes the hunts or prey used. I believe that someone is getting big money for the privilege of hunting humanoid animals, that would be us, Queen."

Breanna was furious, but she listened as she began to realize that she was not a victim of a mistake.

Ace continued, "When the hunt happens, most prey are killed, sometimes however the hunted are lucky as was my case. I survived the hunt and took some hunters out in the process. This elevates me to a higher rank of prey to be hunted by more experienced hunters next time around. Someone determined that you would be paired with experienced prey rather than the normal first-time prey which are generally killed quickly, as the joker will be." He looked over his shoulder at the shivering heap, "Right Joker?" The Joker just continued to sob without acknowledging Ace.

"The way I figure this situation is that my former business partner, Tatiana paid a fee for me to become prey. I hate to say it, but your husband must have paid a higher fee to insure you were hunted by more experienced hunters to ensure less chance of survival. I guess that he believes that you are a fighter. Keeping that in mind, I'm asking you. Are you ready to fight for your life?"

She just nodded, but the fury in her eyes spoke volumes.

"If you work with me, I might be able to save both our arses, but if you don't, I won't risk my life for you. On this planet, it is kill or be killed. Do you understand? From here on out, as long as we speak quietly and calmly, the watchers won't pay attention to the conversation." Cameron was wrong in that assumption; the watchers knew all things.

"There are rules about the hunt, our trackers will be turned off. That is our 'sporting chance' and the watchers are not allowed to reveal conversations or plans shared amongst the hunters or the prey. I believe that the watchers are gamblers. Do not eat any food that appears to be processed. In the field, we will eat only vegetation or freshly killed animals. I'm sorry to tell you that we will have no fire, so the meat will be raw, but you will need it to keep your strength. This will be a three-day hunt and you won't have enough strength to survive on vegetation alone. Do you understand all that I've told you?' She nodded in silent affirmation.

"Watchers? Trackers?" asked Breanna very quietly.

"Yes", Ace pointed to small monitoring devices in every interior corner of the room. Each device had its tiny red-light indication showing its 'working' condition.

"I see, do you have reason to believe that they want us to lose? Is the deck stacked against us?", she asked.

"Queen, I can't answer that with authority, but I'm thinking of a way to try to find out. I will begin to show you some hand signals, the ability to communicate silently is integral to survival."

And so, the training in hand signals began. King joined in the training and collaboration. Joker was a first-time prey and all he could do was hug his knees in the corner sobbing silently. The Joker had no idea how he had landed in the prey bay, the only thing he thought he knew was that he didn't have a snowball in hell chance of surviving.

Ace didn't have all the answers. He didn't know why he was in the prey group for a novice hunt – this group had two experienced and two sacrificial prey. He suspected, however, that the reason for this arrangement was a cheating bookie's attempt to rig the betting odds. Maybe the presence of a woman in the prey was the reason they gave her two warriors. If this concept was right, he and the King would have a better chance of surviving by protecting the Queen.

They had no idea that the team roster had been provided to David which incentivized him to send some discrete bribes to the hunters to focus on the female of the prey. The additional time provided Ace, King, and the Queen more opportunity for strategic planning to prepare for the next hunt. The watchers were advised of the bribes, so their response was to allow the prey team two days to strategize.

Breanna asked, "So why would I not eat anything processed?"

"In my previous hunt, one of the prey found and ate what he thought was food left behind by the hunters. It was poisoned. From what I've learned from seasoned prey is that there are some rules. Apparently, a hunter gets a single advantage, so one of them got a poison as his or her weapon advantage."

Breanna: "I don't suppose the prey gets an advantage?"

"I can't explain why or who determines this, but it seems like each prey has a different advantage. I have reason to believe that my tracker was truly off because the hunters seemed to have radar on the others when all the trackers were supposed to be off. I felt like I survived by being invisible, which gave me opportunities to lay some traps for the hunters. I'm sure I killed or injured at least two of the four, then managed to hide until the expiration time of the hunt. I'm not gonna claim to know everything, Queen, just that I've learned some survival techniques and much good information about the terrain."

The hunt began and as predicted, the Joker was killed within 40 minutes, while the King lasted two full days before losing his balance and crashing through deadfall revealing his presence. Ace and Queen survived the first hunt. Breanna had followed directions from Ace to the letter and they had only moved during the daytime while staying undercover in a cave known to Ace from his previous experience. Breanna had no idea what the meat was and didn't wish to know. She had eaten only the vegetation that Ace had approved for its safety while declining the raw meat he offered. Their survival had been a result of Ace's experience despite the more experienced hunters. Breanna had learned stealth and agility in addition to a familiarity with the landscape and terrain. Staying undercover was the easiest part with Ace helping her to stay invisible. The scariest part for Breanna was her first sighting of a Swalk.

* * *

Only a few days had passed before settling into his office, when David got the E-comm from his I.O.T.A.A. contact about Breanna.

"David, I'm sorry to bring news of your wife Breanna."

"Finally!!" Thought David, until he read on.

"Breanna was released into the hunt with three men. Two men lost their lives in the hunt. The 3rd and Breanna are missing."

His response:

"WHAT the hell?! Missing? What about their trackers?"

He checked his schedule and knew that he must find out what went wrong on Hephaestus, he would need to organize a 'Prize' hunt himself. She will not escape a 'for-profit hunt'. He sent off another message to his I.O.T.A.A. contact:

"Keep prey in Holding – arrange for special high credit prize hunt – only highly experienced hunters allowed. Credits will be deposited directly. Decorum would prevent me from joining the hunt. AND TURN THE PREY TRACKERS ON!!! I'm good with the additional fees."

David quickly realized he was going to need to cover his bases before Breanna was entered into the second hunt. So, he began preparing E-comms to be sent at regular intervals to her Earth address. Each message was filled with words of love and concern as to why she hadn't arrived here on Mercari. He composed messages stating his plans for their romantic reunion. The words made him feel slightly nauseous to write, especially now that he knew she had somehow survived the hunt which should have terminated her life.

While David Arthur was arranging the promotion of the special one-week-long, two-million credit prize hunt which would only be open to professional hunters on Hephaestus, Ace and Breanna were developing their own hunt. The watchers knew that the two were strategizing but they also had a plan. They were indeed gamblers and they had earned a lot of credits on the previous hunt by betting on these two. They knew that the next hunt was going to be stacked with professionals, that there were prize credits involved, so these two weren't going to do so well without a bit of inside help. The hunters were favored to win, the watchers needed to control the odds if they hoped to make money on the upcoming hunt.

* * *

That afternoon when Ace and the Queen were served their lunches, there was a small piece of paper stuck under the cover over the food. Ace noticed it immediately and quickly spirited it into his pocket. "Be right back Queen, need to take a quick trip to the loo…"

When he returned to the table, he whispered to Breanna, "we have a benefactor."

Breanna looked around the room – nothing had changed in there. He whispered again, "we are getting a team partner, Jack".

"Jack?"

"Yes, my Queen – Jack of all trades and technologies."

"As in, a QR programmer?"

"Ahhhh, the Queen is smart as she is beautiful."

Then Ace loudly proclaimed, "This warming unit is not working properly in here. Could the prey that are about to die at least have a technician who can program the bleeding warmer device to work properly before they are murdered in the hunt??? For bloody sake, if I had a tablet, I'd order some FRPs!" His loud proclamation was theatrical as he walked slowly in a circle with his hands flailing in the air for emphasis on his 'frustration'. The monitor on the wall blinked off – only for a second but he knew that his request was acknowledged. They would be getting a programmer and someplace there would be a tablet.

"Might as well go for broke" he thought as he walked to the little warmer device. With his finger on the glass, he traced the letters 'L O O'. They were both watching the monitor as he spelled LOO. The monitor blinked off, just a second, but no doubt the message had been received. And Queen Arthur understood what the message meant also. They were going to get a tablet in the restroom before they were released to the hunt, and they were going to have a programmer hacker as a teammate. Ace made the sign of the cross and the monitor blinked off, just for a second. It was his 'thank you' to the watchers.

Ace and the Queen returned to their meal and strategy, they needed a plan to keep the Jack-of-all-trades alive long enough to reprogram the QRs and at the same time keep from getting killed by professionals. It was going to be a long night…

VARMUS

For twenty-six years Dr. Xi Woo had worked diligently to establish his esteemed career. Unfortunately for some aspiring doctors in his sphere, it had been necessary to eliminate his opposition using the employment of some 'medical accidents' in the laboratory to remove the 'would-be' competition for the coveted position of W.H O. director. He had come from a long line of faithful communists within the Chinese elite families. Even prestige and money couldn't buy such a position, so he worked hard, and eliminated contenders along the way.

His achievements in laboratories across the entire country of China, as well as the USA CDC, were renowned in the scientific communities. His attention to safety measures protected him from the deadly viruses of the Earth and continuously allowed him to move forward toward his goal. It seemed that, finally, he was about to get the title he had literally killed for. He sat patiently at the first table with the Chinese President Tang Chi, flanked by his competition Dr. Ya Tong who was also awaiting the announcement.

Following a glowing introduction, President Chi rose to

the podium. Dr. Woo held his breath as he waited for the announcement of his name until he realized that the President was announcing that the most honorable recipient of the position of Director of the W.H.O. was Dr. Ya Tong. Woo couldn't believe his ears!!! Tong proudly stepped to the microphone to make a long-winded acceptance speech as President Chi returned to the table to shake the hand of Dr. Woo.

"Mr. President," he hissed, "I don't understand…. I most humbly ask how Tong is received as the WHO Director. The position is one that I've worked hard to obtain."

The President raised his glass to Woo as he quietly said, "Dr. Woo. I would not suggest such a lowly position on Earth for you when your talent is so much more suited to the position of Head of Universal Research. To your most good fortune you are now the head of epidemiology on Planet Varmus. We have much to discuss, my friend. We have great plans for our beloved China. Varmus has much to offer to elevate the position of China to finally control the Earth. You will be the instrument of the long-awaited rise of the Dragon, my dear friend Woo."

The following afternoon, Dr. Woo met with President Tang Chi to discuss the plans for Varmus.

"As you know, my friend Woo, Varmus is a quarantined planet. Only the most trusted and knowledgeable doctors and researchers are permitted to go there. We have worked for several years to secure this opportunity for you. China has aspired to be a world power for generations. Finally, with your directorship on Varmus, we will have the opportunity to acquire the most lethal biological material from throughout the universe. The laboratories will be under your control where you will determine the biological agents which will be most useful to refine and use to finally eliminate our adversaries in the United States forever. Already, we have facilitated a separate arrival port for disposable human research subjects. They will be sent as lab assistants but held in containment facilities until needed for your testing purposes. Congratulations, Dr. Woo. You hold the key to the fulfillment of the ancient Chinese dream in your hands."

Woo was still speechless after President Tang's words, so the President continued.

"Next week, you will be transported from Dongguan GaliPort to Varmus, where you will be escorted to your residence after a tour of the campus. Please take your leave to say goodbye to friends and family during this coming week and compile a short list of lab assistants that you trust to join you. Of course, you will finalize your list once on Varmus, after assessing the laboratory facilities. Be aware that there will be other doctors on Varmus, some from Earth, which you may choose to use and dispose of if not trustworthy. There will also be alien researchers and aides. You have complete control, however, so take caution in organizing your researchers. Do you have any questions for me, Dr. Woo?"

Dr. Woo only wanted to know if he would be prevented from ever returning to planet Earth.

"Oh, you will have your opportunity to return to see the glory of China ruling the Earth, Dr. Woo!"

So, with the most respectful bow to the President, Dr. Woo backed from the office and went to begin his preparations to leave. What an amazing opportunity for Woo. On Varmus, he would not be limited to studying and mutating the most dangerous bacteria known on Earth, but from the entire universe! This was an opportunity that he could have only dreamed of.

He knew that the safety measures on Varmus were surely the most stringent ever known, but he would find a way to choose the perfect bacteria to modify and selectively destroy the only enemy that prevented China from gaining full economic control of the entire planet.

He had little to do in China before his departure. Family, friends, and colleagues meant nothing when compared to the opportunity to control the world. Dr. Woo could have no moment of sleep until he departed for Dongguan GaliPort. He was drunk with the power gifted to him by the President.

TERRAORA

The E-brochure showed photos of handsome homey residences for the miners of TerreOra planet. The images were distributed to target groups of working and unemployed miners. Planet Earth had more than one disadvantage for miners. There were too many people needing too much space and a decreased volume of products extracted. The mines got smaller and less productive as Earth gave reduced yields. The wages promised on TerreOra were lucrative compared to the competitive controlled wages imposed on Earth. Images showed mothers with children in playgrounds and men running state-of-the-art mining equipment. As the material got more widely distributed, the miners began to discuss the move with their wives. Further discussion and investigation referred prospective employees to fill out the E-applications which would be processed by D. Arthur Enterprises, Mercari campus. The application included the standard questions about work history, salary requirements, and general health conditions. There was a separate form for the wife, if applicable, which required a gynecological evaluation. The brief explanation for the examination requirement stated that currently there was a limited number of maternity facilities which would be increased in the future. For this reason, a wife could not be pregnant at the time of transport.

The application had check boxes for the type of work desired. In addition to mining, there were construction builders, butchers, cooks, and childcare provider check boxes. Maternity medical service providers were also sought but referred to a different link, as these positions would be near-future opportunities.

The miners quickly began to fill out applications, while the wives and girlfriends scheduled OB/GYN appointments in countries across the world. David Arthur Enterprises needed to hire a staff to manage the influx of miners and he had to make sure that the single miners arrived first, as they could be housed in men's quarters which were basically retrofitted warehouses for the exhausted men. The natives were enlisted to build more housing, which would be slightly better for the married employees.

When the new employees began to arrive, they were most often disappointed at the lodging but could see that new construction was underway and the warehousing of men was just a temporary situation. They went to work and earned their pay and fell asleep on the thin cots, often in their work clothing because they were too exhausted to do anything else.

The food was different from Earth. It seemed to be a sort of stew, short on vegetables but abundant in protein that was quite tasty, so there were no complaints to the culinary providers there. Only the butchers knew that the source of the protein was deceased natives and overworked miners. The bones were cooked down to make a great broth and the meat was always tender. Mr. Arthur had even imported pallets of spices for the kitchen staff to ensure that the mystery meat was enjoyable to all.

Work-life was hard for a miner, but the pay was good and so too, the food. None of them questioned what they would use the credits for, it was all on their records, how much they were earning. If they asked for some to be sent back to a family member, there were fast records indicating that the transfer was made. The miners never thought about their inability to communicate with Earth. They accepted the suggestion that the TerreOra planet core prevented good communication signals. It was explained to them that the financial transactions to other planets needed to be done through secure GaliWorm containers, which often caused delays, but they could rest assured that transactions were always completed.

By the time the married men were allowed to transport to TerreOra, the family residences had been built, they were small, very small. The women were allowed to buy protein and spices from the company store with credits so they could do their own cooking, but the food wasn't any better than that which had been refined by the months of local culinary experimentation. Over the months, DAE began to import produce, at grossly inflated prices, to the DAE company stores where credits would be transferred from the miners' accounts back to the David Arthur coffers.

Married couples were financially incentivized to bear children. Indiscriminate relationships were considered criminal and subject to ejection from TerreOra back to the home planet. But not wanting information about this planet shared, the transgression ejection transport was rescheduled to Hephaestus for use as prey or Varmus for medical research studies depending on the bid price for the subject. A low bid could send the offender to the TerreOra feed warehouse rather than through the GaliPort.

There was a maternity clinic equipped with sophisticated technology which could very quickly determine the sex of a fetus. If the fetus was a female, the mother would urgently need to be moved to a facility to 'save the child' because the clinicians would claim a dire medical need for constant evaluation during the pregnancy. During the gestation period of the female child, the mother would be fed special vitamins which were growth hormones to accelerate the maturation process of the fetus. This acceleration was unknown to the mother and of course, the mother would do what was best for the child. Though a mother would be rushed to a facility where the special vitamins were infused through the mother's blood, the result always seemed to be the same. In the end, the female child 'didn't survive the delivery' and the mother went home to her husband childless to try again. There was no option for a burial service or final viewing. The sedated mother was immediately removed to her quarters with her husband to grieve the loss.

The only known surviving infants, of the miners, were the male ones who grew up to become miners. The females that survived birth, were raised in a remote location and monitored for their vital statistics to be transported to Eros at the time of puberty. For the genetically inferior, there was the feed lot or off to Hephaestus to the prey bin in the case of particular agility or strength. On rare occasions, a young woman was allowed to stay to be a caregiver in the girl-child compound. No girl-child ever saw a male other than the native non-human males who were not recognizable as male. This compound had been operational for about twenty years and had proven effective in preventing the overpopulation of the planet.

If a woman conceived only female infants, she would generally 'die from childbirth complications' often before her change happened. The women who delivered male children were allowed to continue delivering until they neared the time when the change of life would prevent further pregnancies. The clinicians carefully monitored the women to ensure that even male-bearing women would end up with a 'childbirth complication' to take the woman's life as she approached her change.

Planet management had considered applying a medical procedure to all fetuses to insure only male infants were delivered. Though this could have been easily accomplished with genetic modification, there was a lucrative financial asset factor in the decision to allow some female births. TerreOra was not going to become an overcrowded planet like Earth. The planned life expectancy of a female on TerreOra was forty-five. Males usually lasted to the ripe old age of sixty unless they suffered health issues.

The D Arthur Enterprises would never be paying retirement funds. His profit margin was extraordinary as the miners' earnings credits were never spent, but merely held in DAE holdings. His overhead was small and profit margins on the exports were large. D Arthur was an extremely wealthy man.

When, on the off chance, the clinicians of the maternity clinic delivered a female child, protocol steps were taken to remove the child to the remote area referred to as the girl-child compound. The equipment used in the early pregnancy diagnostics was technologically outstanding when properly calibrated and maintained. Occasionally accidents happened and an expected female child turned out to be a male at the time of delivery. This was a rare occurrence, so the clinicians simply opted to castrate the now-girl-child and send it off to the girl-child compound. The 'he-male' would be raised as a female but obviously not suitable for purposes of transport to breeding planets. This had been the case with Apolonika. Her parents, whom she'd never known, had been from an Earth African tribe, or so she was told, she had been coached to enhance her Amazonian size and strength through hard work and nutritious food. The staff of the girl-child compound knew that her options would be Varmus to be used as a medical lab animal or Hephaestus to be hunted. She was a handsome woman and they had over the years, encouraged her to become the magnificent masculine specimen with aggressive skills and lightning reaction that would enhance her chances of survival in a hunt, which, as luck would have it, became her destiny.

At age seventeen, she had been selected for an upcoming event where she would become part of the prey team with Ace, Queen, and Jack. She would be dubbed by the betting community as King, a tribute to her predecessor who had survived for 48 hours of a 72-hour hunt.

THE HUNT — PLANNING

The Japanese geek had tried to apply to be a hunter in this event, but David had called in a favor and accepted the geek after having his status changed from hunter to prey. The idea that the Japanese application, so clearly fabricated to liken the applicant to an accomplished Professional hunter, would not draw attention to the question of its authenticity, was ludicrous. In David's opinion, this diminutive guy, Ming Tsu, later to be referred to in the betting pool as Jack, would be the first to die. He would not risk allowing a non-experienced computer programmer to be included on a hunt team dedicated to the final destruction of Breanna.

Of course, when the day of the hunt had arrived, David Arthur could not risk being there considering that his wife was amongst the prey. The viewing audience would not know that it was he who had financed the prize and selected the male hunters for the event. He would have a female selected from the TerreOra girl-child compound, young enough to die quickly. He was leaving nothing to chance. The E-comm delay prevented him from getting accurate numbers of the betting odds against the prey team as well as individual odds for and against the hunt party.

There was betting on how long a participant would last, how long it took each one to die, and the method of death; the betting opportunities seemed to be limitless.

The worst part was the E-comm delay, which would deny him the immediate joy of knowing that she was finished, and the video delay would not provide him with the joy of watching her die via live feed. He hoped that she would try to seduce a hunter before she was killed. She had always used her body to control men.

One last time, he considered taking the GaliPort over there to watch the hunt on a big screen monitor in 'real-time'. But he knew the risk of his presence was greater than the pleasure he'd receive from being there.

EARTH — JAPAN

Ming Tsu was probably a genius. He was an intellectual giant despite his 4'11" height. His life had been devoted to the study of all things that would compensate for his 'vertical challenge'. He excelled in the study of physics, electronics, mechanics, biology, and virtually all sciences. He had a photographic memory, so he spent his life consuming information that he was able to spontaneously recall when needed to solve any problem. To his benefit, he studied the sciences of psychology and the new and ancient military strategies of warring people throughout the ages of recorded history.

The thing he enjoyed most of all was his ability to hack into electronic data systems to, occasionally, create a little chaos. He didn't do it for credits even though it could have been a lucrative business. He was a simple man with simple tastes which he easily funded with a legal consulting firm where he was employed to develop solutions for companies with inefficient organizational issues. Recently, however, he had been hacking on a particularly intriguing test of his chaotic skills, during working hours, and the company for which he worked terminated his services based on their zero-tolerance policy about using company equipment for personal use.

His sudden employment status was not a concern, he'd saved his whole 'simple' life, so he decided that he would use some of his credits to buy into a hunting trip. The advertisements didn't elucidate what was to be hunted but did specify that it was open only to professionals. "*Well,*" Tsu thought, "*I can easily modify my QR to prove my professional status, and the winning credit purse would more than reimburse me for about a year of lost wages while I decide where I will work upon my return to Earth Japan.*" He spent the afternoon researching the resumes of professional hunters and tailored his application to ensure that he would be considered for the special prize hunt. With that done, he only had to upload the pro-hunt data into his QR which only took seconds. Of course, the following day he received his acceptance for entry to the hunt with the GaliPort destination and time. He spent the remaining earth time consuming more data to ensure that he would be the winner of the hunt.

Tsu watched the monitor count down:

T minus 5…4…3…2…1

Then:

"Welcome to Hephaestus Mr. Ming Tsu – Please enter the doorway to your left to meet your survival team."

"*Survival team?*" thought Tsu. Slight confusion was a common reaction to some GaliPort connections, he'd read that, but "*survival team – as in Prey?!?*"

Through the door to his left was an entry to decontamination which took much less time than the Earth departure process, so he was soon face to face with three camo-clad humans who were his prey team. They all gestured for 'silence' to which he complied. One of his many learned talents was American Sign Language which he quickly taught his team.

He explained to them what he'd read about animal life on Hephaestus. For the most part, there was little that a human could not overcome other than the Swalk. This was an animal similar in size and appearance to a large polar bear, but it walked on two legs – only running on four and able to run about 56.3KPM for a limited time, so it was best to see the Swalk before it saw you. Fortunately, it couldn't run at this speed very long, it was a sprinter, not a distance creature based on its size and weight, which were significant, meaning it was very big. It was an animal that preferred to be left alone but if cornered, it was equipped with a toxin that it could inject through a bite or scratch of its claws. The toxin was not lethal, but able to paralyze the recipient for approximately thirty Earth minutes. The Swalk was an omnivore and 'gatherer' so once the Swalk was constrained or killed, the stored food source would be available to the prey team.

This would save them a great deal of time. He didn't think that it would be necessary to eat the Swalk meat, but the killing and skinning of one might provide warmth from its pelt during the six nights they would be without a heat source. The team had agreed the risk of making a fire was too great. They didn't know if the hunters would have battery-operated heating modules for their nights. They would find out after their first kill but agreed it best to plan on possibly getting a pelt or two for comfort.

Ace had not seen one on either of his hunts, so this was valuable information for their strategy. He asked in the newly learned sign language if Tsu, now dubbed Jack, had learned where these Swalk lived or their sleeping habits. Great question for Jack Tsu, the Swalk were foragers and night creatures preferring to sleep in small shallow rocky caverns. Apolonika got involved in the discussion of the

Swalk. She was good at braiding strong flexible ropes from grass fiber. These ropes would be well suited for the quick constraint of the claws of the Swalk to milk the toxin. The toxin could then be applied to spear weapons and blow darts to be employed against the hunters.

With the new knowledge of the Swalk, Ace remembered seeing shallow caverns near the edges of high cliffs. He and the Queen had even used some of them for hiding. "*It was a good thing,*" he thought," *that we hadn't entered one that was occupied.*" Perhaps if there was sufficient time after milking a Swalk, they might push it off the cliff to its sleepy death which would provide the team a safe shelter.

In the wee hours when the prey team should be sleeping, they continued their strategizing. Ace advised Jack that they were expecting to receive a tablet, so Jack was mentally planning the QR revisions for each of them. Breanna had ideas about what she'd like Jack to do about David when the hunt was done but decided not to get ahead of the more pressing plan of surviving the seven-day hunt before them.

Ace and the Queen regularly checked the loo and finally discovered the tablet which was spirited into the personal room. This tablet was given at the end of the day to Jack Tsu for his nighttime program efforts. Using the tablet, he was able to get satellite images of the hunt area and he searched for heat signatures to find and map the locations of several Swalk and their caverns. The Swalk were nocturnal, but this allowed Jack to track their forage habits and territories. He found that they had distinct travel patterns and perimeters which he committed to memory and marked a map on the tablet to show the rest of the team.

For some unknown reason, the synthetic eating utensils they had been receiving were replaced with metal ones which they quickly stowed and turned into weapons in the silent nighttime. When the metal utensils appeared, Jack gave Ace his meal tray and in return, Ace bowed from the waist in a gesture of thank you to Jack Tsu. His exaggerated bow was met with a brief blink on the monitor. His gratitude to the watchers was acknowledged.

Apolonika had been busily stripping the sleeves and legs from her sturdy camo uniform fabric. The strips she used for her braiding project. The modified uniform would leave her scantily clad, but for Apolonika, less clothing equaled increased mobility. The sturdy bindings would be easily concealed until they were needed in the hunt.

During one of their lunchroom strategy planning sessions, Ace raised the issue of possible hunter replacements. He loudly said, "Does anyone here think there is a possibility that quick destruction of hunters would shorten the length of the hunt?" The prey watched the monitor – no blink.... "*Damn*," thought Ace. So, he posed his question differently. He said – "Does anyone believe that the hunt could be ended on Day five?" They watched the monitor intensely, One blink.

"OKAY then, since you all don't have a clue, how about we say our goal is to eliminate the last hunter on Day five. We are gonna need to think of some sort of more robust device for our blow dart guns than the lunch sipping straws."

One blink.

An hour later, a plumber arrived to work on a fitting in the LOO. Apparently, he forgot to remove the extra pipe sections that happened to be just the right size to make sturdy blow guns.

Ace raised his arms and loudly said, "Guess the watchers took pity on our leaky loo. Wish there was a way to thank them." He looked at the monitor.

One blink.

So, Ace gestured his slow theatrical bow to the monitor.

The blow guns were manufactured from the secreted Loo plumbing parts provided by their watcher benefactors.

The darts, spears, and trident heads were built from the cutlery change – thanks to the watchers. The prey weapons were sewn into the camo clothing awaiting the day of the hunt.

Two days later would be the opening day of the hunt. The betting bookies were raking in credits from across the universe. The planets knew there would be a delay in receiving the video of the hunt, but the betting had been going on for over a week. This hunt was the most anticipated broadcast ever planned. Normally hunts weren't promoted beyond Hephaestus, but this one had been widely promoted because of the very valuable prize credit purse which had incentivized the betting bookies to further promote the event. This hunt was bigger than the old Earth Superbowl fanfare with its high credit advertising campaigns. The viewers on Hephaestus would only be able to see the video after submitting credits for a subscription, but theirs would be live streaming unlike the delayed off-planet broadcast which also required credits to watch. Every hotel, hostile, and spare room on the planet had been rented by travelers who couldn't bear to wait for the delayed videocasts on their own planets. The Hephaestus GaliPort had temporarily suspended the incoming decontamination requirement to accommodate the influx of sports tourism revenue.

The planet controller had quickly determined that, based on the reservations and revenue, the Colossal Hunt would be the first of the future Annual Colossal Hunts. the hunt masters were already developing the applications, including the strict qualifications to become accepted to the ACH II. There was also a team discussing a way to promote a special financial incentive to entice applicants to a Prey lottery. the hunt promoters included professional marketers who were pouring through volumes of photos of shining skinned models bulked over with photo-enhanced muscles dripping with sweat droplets as they held the handmade instruments of their defense against the prey. Oh yes, the promo team knew well that they would be able to entice egotistical hordes of would-be prey. The team marketers knew exactly how to sell advertisements universally. By this time next year, Hephaestus would be one of the wealthiest planets in the universe!

By the time the hunt was ready to proceed, the prey had their fine-tuned plans ready to go. The watchers had been feeding misinformation to the betting community. The result of the misinformation feed was an astronomical rise in the betting odds against the prey. The watchers would soon be extremely wealthy and not even David Arthur would be able to prove any collusion had taken place.

I.O.T.A.A.

THE HUNT — DAY ONE

On planets across the universe, there were Hunt Parties with large groups getting together to watch the videocasts. People wearing costumes fashioned to resemble their favorite contestants. There was no business or service on Hephaestus that was not benefiting from the upcoming 'Hunt of the Century'. The city businesses had windows covered with scrolling E-posters showing photos of the hunters and the prey contestants. the hunters were depicted as handsome, strong, virile men. The prey had been represented by edited photos which made them appear to be emaciated and weak. Even Apolonika, who was, in reality, an amazon of a woman in beauty, strength, and towering height, appeared to have her head attached to a short thin grey-skinned woman. These doctored photos must have been part of the bookie's campaign to keep the odds growth soaring to even greater heights in favor of the hunters.

The live streaming of the hunt was a surprise to the viewing audience, as they saw healthy-looking prey, especially the magnificent Amazonian King Apolonika. The advertised images of the prey team had the women depicted as frail or weak. The male prey had appeared to be lost or confused in the images, especially the Asian one who was indeed small in stature, but not looking confused now.

There was no anxiousness amongst the prey as the time for the hunt approached, they had tailored their plans, often under cover of darkness during their normal sleep periods.

The watchers knew that even though the hunt had been programmed for the prey trackers to be active, the tracking advantage would have no value to the hunters for this game. The tracking program in each prey QR had been modified by Jack Tsu. As the hunters would be looking for their prey using the QR trackers, they would be sent in the exact opposite direction of the actual coordinates. These creative QR modifications would put the hunters at locations that were known in advance by the prey, who would have their traps set before the hunters arrived at the various destinations. This would be a big advantage for prey, Team Straight, as they were now referred to due to their poker game names.

The horns sounded at the beginning of the hunt. It only took seconds for the hunters to engage their prey trackers to observe and record the blinking lights of the four, which quickly separated into two groups. The hunters were disappointed at the absurdity of the group separating. Hunter 1, also known as Buff, stood with hunter 2, Chef, hunter 3, Beef and hunter 4, Stew. They agreed that they would give the prey group, now referred to as the 'Straight', a chance to sprint away some of their energy. It was obvious to the hunters that the Straight had no strategy skills and they were each disappointed that although the prize credits were assured, the win was diminished by the lack of challenge they had anticipated. This hunt was promoted as the most challenging universal hunt ever broadcast and they had each paid an inflated cost to apply, so they had expected to be hunting high-quality prey.

Hephaestus was a planet that resembled the prehistoric state of planet Earth. The land mass was comprised of dense rain forests, waterfalls, rivers, and streams. The abundance of water and unpolluted precipitation provided the ultimate nutrition for the growth of intensely colored plants which grew with no boundaries or interruptions to their life cycles. There were both delicious and deadly varieties of food sources for the mostly small lifeforms that existed in the soft moist soil beneath the deep damp layers of foliage. The water of the planet was derived from the greenhouse effect generated by the photosynthesis process of the plants in this planet's rainforest.

The prey knew where the soil would be soft and easily shaped into pit traps. They knew where the moist reeds were that would easily provide coverage for King Apolonika as she quickly braided the ropes they would need for traps and trip wires. The camo ankle and wrist bindings were tested and proven in advance of the hunt. The long reed ropes would serve other needs.

King, nimble in her scant camo clothing, and the Queen raced to the location of the braiding reeds. She felt that with less clothing, she was more agile than she had been when she trained on TerraOra. Her skin was dark and needed nothing but perhaps a few large leaves tucked into the scant cloth covering her lower parts and the dreads of her hair. The Queen however needed the camo to disguise her very white skin and blonde hair.

Ace and Jack would be digging and preparing the first set of shallow pit traps which were armed with rows of sharp sticks and rocks to inflict injuries as the hunters fell into a pit. With this task done, they joined the Queen and King with the ropes at the designated Swalk den. They knew that the four of them with the rope nooses in hand would be able to quickly hobble the Swalk and milk the toxin for their blow gun darts and spears. Jack had a backup plan for the tablet device to be used as a pseudo-taser device if the Swalk needed to be subdued. This taser plan was a most desperate plan B because they expected that the tablet would be needed for their planetary exit once they had defeated the hunters. Jack's models couldn't predict with 100% accuracy whether the use of the tablet in this manner would destroy the power module.

When the prey team met to subdue the Swalk, the King and Queen would have sufficient ropes and materials for the making of more restraint devices to bind the apprehended hunters. Ace reminded them that if they immediately killed the hunters, there was a chance that the hunt commission could bring in a fresh supply of replacements. The result of this possibility led them to the conclusion that the hunters must be slowed down, captured, and confined until the last day or two of the hunt.

* * *

After what they considered a fair head start for the prey, the hunters checked their advantage trackers which showed two of the prey to be stationary a couple of kilometers away. Beef and Stew chose to track the females, King and Queen. Beef liked the women from a personal perspective and would relish an opportunity with the blonde, but Stew's desire was the Amazon King. He expected that there was much more to her than the doctored photos and more challenges despite her gender. There had even been rumors that King was a castrated male, if this was true, he/she would be much more of a challenge to hunt than the little 'Princess' that was being dubbed Queen. Beef had been advised that extreme brutality of the 'Queen' would bring unpublished rewards coming from a privately interested investor, so he had early on planned that these women would be his primary targets.

Buff and Chef decided to follow suit going after the

male prey and parting ways with Stew and Beef. On the path to their destination, they had set their plan. Chef was to circle behind the pray and flush them from their hiding place while Buff would be ready with his crossbow to take the first one out, Chef could follow and cut the throat of the second one. Once they arrived at the cave where the stationary prey was, Chef stealthily entered. What he found was not the sleeping prey but a sleeping bear-looking creature that did NOT like its sleep interrupted. The Swalk charged at Chef chasing him through the opening of the cave toward Buff. Just moments before the crossbow arrow pierced the head of the Swalk, it took a mighty swipe with its paw toward Chef. Though only grazed by the long sharp claws, the shallow cuts burned like fire just before he dropped to the ground, unable to move.

"*Shit*," thought Buff, "*he's still breathing, so I can't just leave him here in case there are more of these animals around.*" So, he dragged his partner off to a safer clearing where he could wash and wrap the arm. Now that he had time to think through what had happened, he realized that this creature must have some sort of toxin. He also saw that Chef no longer had his hunting knife. He quickly decided that he must return to the cave for the knife.

* * *

Ace and Jack had been behind the cave, just over the edge of the cliff on a ledge. They had heard but not seen the scenario play out. It was easy to tell when the one hunter had dragged the other away. Ace and Jack quickly scrambled over the edge, to find the dead Swalk. The knife was under the Swalk, apparently dropped when it took its swipe at the hunter. They quickly dragged the dead creature to the edge of the cliff, removed its claws with the bonus hunting knife, and pushed it over the edge. The rest of their fast work involved filling a shirt with the food from the cave while Ace covered the tracks of their disposal of the Swalk. These things were done minutes before they departed to rejoin the King and Queen.

When Buff returned to recover the knife, alarm bells sounded in his head. At the cave, he found that both the animal and knife were missing. The absence of these things let him know that in this first encounter, the prey had outsmarted them. He now wondered if the Prey were more than what he had considered being inept and dimwitted. It could be that they were actual adversaries.

Ace and Jack went in another direction to the next soft earth area where they assembled their weapons and dug the next trip pits. These two pits were located within the sprint distance of a currently sleeping Swalk. The locations had been calibrated to ensure that when the hunters went to the caverns, there was a chance that they would fall into the pit while being chased by a disturbed Swalk. Each false movement of the prey had been programmed and uploaded to the hunters' trackers, so the prey now had the advantage of controlling the direction of the hunters. The compromised signals showing a non-strategic split-up of the Team Straight had worked its magic triggering the hunters to split up and choose their desired prey while falling victim to the falsified locations.

With the ropes and binding straps created, the team met at the designated Swalk location just as night began to fall. The arrival of Ace and Jack with the recovered food and knife was a great cause for a silent celebration by the four. The King and Queen showed a variety of ropes and asked the guys to test their strength. Ace and Jack had planned that upon their return, they would provide the knife to the King because they agreed that she was best equipped to handle it. After testing the ropes, Jack made a rather ceremonial-looking presentation of the knife. This gesture hadn't been planned, but it sure looked great on camera!

Team Straight was now camo-painted with mud and

plant leaves and virtually invisible in their surroundings. Their absolute silence was uninterrupted by their use of sign language messaging, allowing them to remain undetectable from the environment.

The Swalk returned with its furry arms loaded with the nocturnal foraged food and quickly curled just inside the cavern to begin its loud snoring — evidence of its sleep. One of the things that Apolonika had suggested and implemented was a rock 'blind' in the rear of the cavern. Apolonika offered to take up the position behind the blind. She was fearless from surviving seventeen years in the girl-child compound. She was also the fastest member of the team, so she'd have the best chance to escape unharmed if the Swalk were to turn in the direction of the prey rather than the hunters in front of it. Upon the arrival of the hunters, Beef and Stew, Apolonika would spear the rear of the Swalk with the hope it would react to the presence of the hunters before it.

The plan worked flawlessly. Beef and Stew crept to the cavern, believing their trackers which showed two stationary female prey. Apolonika silently slipped from behind her blind and poked the Swalk which quickly jumped up from its sleep and saw Beef and Stew in front of it. The sprint was on, leading Beef and Stew directly into the pit traps just steps beyond the sprint capacity of the Swalk. Of course, Apolonika had slipped out of the cavern quickly following the beginning of the sprint. The Swalk, being roused from its sleep and subsequently racing into bright sunlight, slowed down. Unable to see or catch its targets, Beef and Stew, it gave up and went back to its cavern.

The team's return to the Beef and Stew pits was tricky. They doubted the Swalk would be so easily subdued after a second awakening, but Team Straight needed to recover the hunters from the pits. The Queen used her blow darts to sedate Beef and Stew from an area just beyond the sprint zone. Ace jumped into the pit to bind and secure the hunters with braided ropes to pull them from the pit while praying that they did not disturb the sleeping Swalk. The Queen and King quickly assembled the transport liters while Ace and Jack dragged Beef and Stew from the pit. The hunters were moved to the deep tunnel that Jack had located before the hunt began. This tunnel housed their confiscated Swalk food, and now, Beef and Stew.

Jack efficiently reprogrammed their QRs and trackers to ensure that the remaining hunters, Buff and Chef, would not find the Team Straight hide out. The Straight was delighted to discover that Beef and Stew had heaters that were turned on after Jack had ensured that they couldn't be tracked. Jack quickly modified Beef's tablet to serve as a taser weapon to control the hunters until it was time to kill them. Team Straight members took shifts keeping the hunters sedated and muzzled using small sacks of foliage to prevent them from calling for help or communicating with each other in the unlikely event that they woke from the Swalk toxins or taser jolts.

* * *

Some of the betting odds shifted, but there had been plenty of credits already paid from the odds against Team Straight. The Universal audience watched with rapt attention at the time of the first kill followed by the ceremonial barbarism. The King had the honor of the first kill, and she quickly painted her face with the blood of the hunter 'Stew' and stripped a piece of flesh from each of his cheeks to eat in front of the recording device before raising her fists in the air in a triumphant gesture of defiance to all would-be hunters.

Day one had provided the deaths of one Swalk and the apprehension of two hunters, one of whom became the first Prey Sacrifice. Team Straight hadn't needed to implement their plan to capture Buff and Chef yet. Those two hunters had done the job for them by foolishly relying on the trackers which put them in territorial proximity to the Swalk. Team Straight had returned after the hunters, and collected the toxin, and some fresh meat to take back to their abandoned Swalk cavern. The capture of Beef and Stew along with these collected items coupled with their reed ropes gave them confidence that they would survive this hunt.

I.O.T.A.A.

THE HUNT — DAY TWO

At midday, one of the hunters called Stew was found dead by Buff and Chef. Stew had a broken neck, but his cheeks had been removed. The video of the killing was provided for all to see on the previously disabled recording device which, now at the time of the first killing, was enabled long enough for another video showing Buff and Chef discovering the body. The video clearly showed King breaking the neck of Stew followed by the violent stripping of the cheeks off the face of the first killed hunter. The viewers breathlessly watched as King devoured a piece of raw cheek — blood running down her chin. The audience had no idea that this killing had been staged, not live, and that the piece of cheek was precooked the evening before on the modified heater. The live transmission was the shocked expressions on the faces of the professional hunters as they found the first deceased member of the hunt team with the missing cheeks. Team Straight chuckled at the irony of this recording they made. The media wanted a show, and this is exactly what they were going to get.

Buff and Chef were a little bit off their game plan as the second day neared its end. The tracking devices had done little more than set them to chasing shadows and false trails. There was no contact with the outside world, so they had no idea that the prey seemed to be in control of what was seen in the hunt broadcast. There had been, in Buff's opinion, too many encounters with the Swalk which should not have been awake during the daytime hours. It appeared that they were being driven by the prey. Chef had gotten a swipe by one earlier and Buff had somehow managed to drag him to safety. Buff waited for Chef's toxin to wear off and when the Swalk left to forage as nighttime arrived, Buff was able to extricate them from the danger zone of the Swalk cave. They had no idea that this humiliating scenario was being broadcast.

They found a thicket to hide in through the night, avoiding another encounter from the marauding Swalk, while they strategized a plan to track the prey. They knew their trackers were useless in providing accurate data on the locations of the Straight, so there was only a slight chance that the prey numbers were diminished.

At the end of Hunt Day Two, Buff and Chef only knew for sure that Stew was dead, and that Beef was now missing. There had been no evidence that any of the Straight had been killed. Buff needed to do some soul searching that night because he wasn't feeling so confident with the way things were going.

THE HUNT — DAY THREE

Day three for Buff and Chef arrived with no nocturnal attacks by the Swalk or the Straight. But during the night, Buff realized that since he didn't have a clue where Beef was, it might be time to dispose of Chef. There were the prize credits to consider, but larger than that was the prestige which was now at stake. Chef had been injured and rescued. Buff, on the other hand, had incurred no serious injury, and he had actually needed to rescue Chef, so in Buff's opinion, it wasn't right that he would share the prize credits with the rescued huntsman called Chef.

Buff pondered the situation and rationalized reasons for the actions he knew he needed to take. The prey was a team. The only thing they had to gain or lose was their lives. In the case of the hunters, there was only one prize to be shared with the survivors. He had thought about this deep into the night. The prey had proven to be illusive, but he had confidence that the Straight, however many of them were left, could not match his kill skills. He'd made some strategic mistakes. He had agreed to work as a team, and he had relied on the accuracy of the trackers. Buff now reasoned that Chef was a burden. He would no longer use the tracker. Chef wasn't a bad guy, but he was a liability. and today, Chef would be going swimming from the cliff, a dive not to survive. It was a fact that the hunters shared the prize, so logic dictated that Buff intended to become the sole survivor in this hunt.

As Chef slept off the toxin hangover from last night, Buff left to find the nearest Swalk cave beside the highest cliffs. He set a trip wire parallel to the edge of the cliff and upon his return, he crushed with his boot heel, the tracker they had been using.

In the morning, when Chef looked for the tracker, Buff incredulously asked if Chef didn't remember the Swalk stomping on the tracker? Buff assured him that his was still operational, and he had already located the sleeping prey so they must quickly get there before the Straight did another disappearing act. He told Chef that he understood why he would be apprehensive about going near the Swalk cavern, so he suggested that Chef take up a position at a distance between the cavern and the cliff with his crossbow.

He situated Chef exactly where he needed him to be, then silently crept into the cavern where there were no prey – only a sleeping Swalk which Buff poked from behind driving the creature directly at Chef who, as planned, tripped the wire sending him tumbling over the edge of the cliff to his death. Buff quickly slipped out of the cavern behind the Swalk in pursuit of Chef. He had not, however, counted on the intellect of the Swalk. The angry Swalk turned back when Chef went off the cliff, only to discover another hunter. The Swalk sprinted the short distance driving Buff directly into the pit trap that Ace and Jack had dug the night before, after Buff's visit to set the trip wire planned to send Chef to his death.

This pit dug and armed by Ace and Jack, had pointed stakes awaiting Buff or Chef. The pit wasn't deep, but its stakes penetrated limbs and vital organs. Buff's death was painful and slow as he bled out in the shallow pit. His only thought of salvation was that the Swalk didn't seem interested in eating him alive. He attempted to send a signal on his tracker device, but he did not know that the message was rerouted by a Jack of all trades. The promoters never received an emergency signal. Now the one remaining hunter was bound and being relentlessly tortured by Breanna. Tomorrow would see her victory dance.

I.O.T.A.A.

THE HUNT — DAY FOUR

In the morning, as the Swalk were sleeping, Team Straight had to separate to set more traps. There was only one captive hunter left, but Ace and Jack felt compelled to continue the charade, in case the hunt Commission decided to bring reinforcements.

It was Queen Breanna who stayed behind with Beef. It gave her great pleasure to tighten his bonds while he was sleeping the sleep of the Swalk toxin, but she enjoyed allowing him to come awake long enough to dance a strip tease before him. She'd done it many times to get things she wanted from David, now she fully understood the strength of her sexuality as she used it to torture the wanton Beef. Teasing, never pleasing — always just out of possible grasp and suffering as his scrotum bulged with the unfulfilled need she created with her dance and exploration of her own body in front of him. Then, poking him with the toxin tipped spear returning him to sleep and dreams of the needs that would never be satisfied.

When the afternoon of the 4th day came, the Straight, transported the sleeping Beefcake, as Breanna now referred to the hunter, to the two large hanging trees equipped with bindings for arms and legs. She had teased and tortured him for three days now and he would be the final kill, but the video would not be released until the fifth day of their victory. The temporary decommissioning of the cameras allowed the Straight to provide the illusion of a continuing hunt which was done.

Once Beefcake was strung up by wrists and ankles in a spread-eagle position, naked as a newborn for all the universe to see, Jack released the video of Beefcake crying like a baby as Breanna castrated his no longer erect organ. Breanna and Apolonika danced in victorious barbarous circles around the now-screaming 'warrior-no-more' who begged for relief from his agony.

Ace and Jack knew they dare not put Beefcake out of his misery and deny the King and Queen the pleasure of their victory. So, they waited painfully for permission to dispatch the final hunter. In the end, it was Breanna who took the spear with no toxin and plunged it deep into the chest to kill the final hunter nicknamed Beefcake.

THE HUNT — FINAL DAY

The four-member prey team had survived the hunt. The video broadcasts showed the slow-motion death of Buff, as he bled to death in the pit. The production crew looped the barbaric war dance of the King and Queen and the close-up view of the castrated and agonizing hunter called Beef.

As the horns blew the official end of the hunt, the four of the prey went directly to the nearest video station. As they raised their arms with clenched fists, Breanna delivered a message to the infinitesimal universe.

"I have a message for the females of all the planets of the universe regardless of size or species! There is no need to be dominated by the males of the universe. We will no longer allow ourselves to be used as breeding stock and cast away like the uneaten food on the plate or rotting garbage that is not even consumed by the lowest of low animals of the universe.

For millennium, we have accepted the premise that we are not as intelligent, that we are weaker than the males of our species. We have been demeaned and castigated for so long that we have forgotten the value of our bodies and minds. Today we cry out for the injustice against all females of ages past and present and claim to those of the future that we will no longer accept the domination we have endured. Starting today we shall universally defy dominance and disrespect. Let us together begin to right the wrong, as we are the true strength and honesty of the universe!"

EROS

Angie's quarantine quarters were relatively comfortable, despite the now burdening abdomen housing the rapidly growing fetus. She hadn't asked for a tablet or means to communicate with her husband James. She hadn't figured out how to explain the accidental pregnancy which had happened only days before she departed Earth to join him and begin their own family. There was no valid excuse for her infidelity and though it had crossed her mind to inquire about terminating the pregnancy, she quickly abandoned the idea.

Shortly before the completion of her pregnancy, a counselor came to her to discuss her options regarding the female child she carried. The counselor told her that James had made many inquiries over the weeks about the whereabouts of his wife. She also said that after much counseling with him, the counselor didn't believe that James would be able to agree to share in the raising of the illegitimate child. But, said the counselor, this was only speculation based on psychological profiles done on James. Finally, she suggested considering that since she and James loved each other so much, the best thing might be to give the child up to be raised by another family who was still unable to conceive. Angie was emotionally crushed about the idea of giving up the child, but the reality of the situation was that she had NO idea who it was that had impregnated her. She could have been sexually used by more than one person that night! After some sleepless consideration, she agreed to sign the papers to give the child for adoption immediately at birth. The counselor told her that she should be at peace with the decision because the child would be loved by both adoptive parents and the bonus was that Angie's fertility was established now, so she and James should be able to conceive and have a child together before the year was done.

As the contractions began the delivery process, she was sedated. When she awoke, there was no child, and she was in a facility that had long rows of beds with crying women. "Why," she asked, "are they crying?" The answer came from one of the women, "Because we are now part of the breeding program of Eros too." Hearing this information, Angie fainted again.

When she woke, she found that she was restrained in the bed with an IV tube in her arm. She had no idea how long she had been 'out of it' but she saw a movement under the sheet... As she tried to focus out of the drug-induced semi-coma, she realized the movement under the sheet was her abdomen, and she recognized the feeling of fetal kicking and the tenderness of swollen milk-filled breasts. "Good God, what is happening to me?"

She had been intravenously fed and impregnated while being kept semi-conscious. Now she remembered the crying women and the words 'breeding program'. A nurse arrived, there had been a delay in administering the drug. Angie shouldn't be awake yet.

"WHY?" she asked the nurse – "HOW am I pregnant?? Where is my husband?"

"Your husband is part of the male breeding program as

you are part of the female breeding program."

"Is the child in me created by my husband?'" Angie begged to know.

The nurse laughed, "None of your offspring were created by your husband! Genetic breeding programs would never allow your eggs to be inseminated by a human! You must return to your sleep now; the delivery of the hybrid is difficult for a human incubator."

"WAIT at least tell me how often this will happen?'" demanded Angie.

"You have delivered fourteen hybrid lifeforms so far with no complications. Your body is a great incubator. You will have many more. Sleep now Mrs. Drummond. The delivery is soon to come."

Angie fainted again before the injection into the IV put her into a deep sleep that would protect her from the trauma of delivering the multi-tentacled hybrid lifeform. The alien hybrid was quickly removed to the Eros nursery where it would be sold. Her stimulated egg production had been harvested for immediate use. She would be re-inseminated within the week. She was an asset to the breeding program. The genetic testing on earth had determined her candidacy for the program and it had not been wrong!

Fortunately for James, he never knew what was being done to his wife. His ability to produce viable sperm had quickly diminished to the point that his name had been added to the list of men who would be transported to the feed lots of TerreOra. He'd noticed that he had been receiving much more food lately and he had gained a lot of weight in the last few weeks. "*Maybe the weight gain is the reason I am having this erectile dysfunction,*" he thought, "*I need to start working out and shed a few pounds.*"

He was told that he would be transported to a location where he and Angie would be able to be reunited. After the decontamination procedure, he stepped into the GaliPort chamber.

Displayed on the monitor he saw:

T minus 5...4...3...2...1

And then:

> **"Welcome to TerreOra, Mr. James Drummond, Please step through the doorway to your left where you will be escorted to your quarters."**

And now James Drummond was in the prisoner feed lot warehouse area of TerreOra. His wife's body would continue to be used as an incubator as long as it was physically capable. There would be many varieties of hybrids to accommodate the needs of the weakened civilizations under threat of extinction. Many planets were dying from foreign bacteria which had traveled throughout the universe despite the stringent decontamination processes associated with the increased use of the GaliPort.

VARMUS — DOCTOR XI WOO

Doctor Woo was highly motivated now that he had been established in the laboratory on planet Varmus. The lab campus spanned dozens of miles of land. The security systems were the most advanced technology in the universe with multiple layers of backup systems. The bacteria and viruses were separated into blocks based on their level of lethality. The coding ranged from LEVEL 1 to LEVEL 13 with LEVEL 13 being the most lethal in the universe.

The 'Bug Building' was arranged like a twelve spoked wheel with the twelve corridors being isolated from each other. Each corridor had its own increasing level of protection and security. The center of the 'Bug Building' wheel was only accessible from the roof of the building through a transport tube into the separately powered and contained clean room laboratory surrounded by the individually isolated compartments containing the LEVEL 13 materials.

There were only three doctors on Varmus with security clearance to enter the LEVEL 13 lab. Each of the three had their personalized safety gear. This gear was sterilized after each use and incinerated and replaced once each Varmus month cycle. The laboratory guidelines dictated that there could never be more than one doctor in the LEVEL 13 lab at any given time.

Over the months, Woo had evaluated each of the LEVEL 13 viruses to determine which would meet his plan to decimate a population in five days. He had worked tirelessly to ensure that the selected virus would create a short-lived epidemic with no mutation possibility. The virus would be aerially spread quickly and destroyed with the death of its host.

One of the three doctors with access to LEVEL 13 was an American, Doctor Robert West, with credentials and experience which rivaled Woo's. Woo quickly decided that the good Doctor West would be the unwitting mule that would carry the virus to destroy the United States. He only needed a key element to complete his master plan. The United States CA Territories GaliPort would need to be disabled for five days after the arrival of the 'carrier mule' named Doctor West.

* * *

Memo:

8, September from the office of Doctor Xi Woo:

Beginning at 0800 hours on 12, Friday, October – Varmus Std time. All research staff will be required to go via GaliPort to their respective planets/countries of origin to be medically evaluated for one week followed by two weeks of vacation. During the time of absence, the laboratories will be subjected to annual security upgrades and maintenance evaluations.

This requirement is based on the mandatory I.O.T.A.A. required annual routine cleaning, software updates, and general maintenance of all GaliPort. Your scheduled appointments will be coordinated with your respective home planets.

The transport and medical evaluations will be paid for by Varmus Laboratories funding. Your medical appointments and travel arrangements will be uploaded to your QRs no later than Wednesday, 11 October. Enjoy your vacation time!

Regards,

Woo

* * *

E-comm Dr. Robert West to Alex West Travel agent I.O.T.A.A. Earth Div:

"Son, I need a favor, a surprise of sorts. I need a QR change done. Current schedule Varmus to Earth CA Territories GaliPort October 12. Change the port to Dongguan on the same date and book your mom to join me, on October 20 for a surprise vacation. I owe her a trip to the Great Wall.

Love Dad"

On October 11, Doctor West put on his lab safety gear which had been infected with the virus before Woo left the dressing area. Woo had engineered the virus with a delay. It would take 48 to 72 hours for the bacteria to shed its spore and begin reproducing in the now infected host.

On October 13, Dr. Woo smiled when he saw reports that the CA Territories GaliPort and GaliWorm had been closed temporarily for Earth's annual maintenance. He didn't think about the lack of information about an epidemic that had destroyed the country. Perhaps there was no media personnel left to report that information.

Woo hadn't bothered to develop an antiviral agent since

the plan was to destroy the population of the United States and eventually mutate to a harmless existence. In the two-year interim, however, the Chinese plan would drive the economic policies to impotence and would ensure China's world dominance.

On October 15 when Dr. Xi Woo stepped out of Dongguan GaliPort, he saw sick and dying everywhere he looked. Doctor Robert West was in quarantine in Dongguan medical center, but it didn't matter, the medical center was infected as was every other location and person in the country. Doctor West's wife didn't get that vacation to China. I.O.T.A.A. had no choice but to decommission the Dongguan GaliPort and sterilize the entire country of China which would not be habitable for the foreseeable future.

POSEIDON

The planet was so named because its surface was approximately 90% water. Food on the planet was grown in hydroponic domes mounted on top of pilings similar to the Earth's oil drilling platforms from long ago. The water was fresh, unlike the oceans of Earth. Poseidon had very few permanent residents because too much time living under the water in domes, called UnderPods, had a way of making a person a bit looney. The scientists didn't bother to research if the cause was psychological, or physical, but what they knew was that if someone spent too long down there, the results were not good. This was the reason that the hydroponic farmers and other business service providers were required to work for one Poseidon year, or less, and be relieved to a different planet with a surface for one year before returning to work. I.O.T.A.A. marketed the planet to those who loved clean clear fresh water. The divers and treasure hunters couldn't get enough of the planet.

The GaliPort was inside a surface dome named the 'GaliDome', that contained a pneumatic elevator system for transport to the underwater decontamination and quarantine UnderPod. Since the planet was covered with water, there were occasional surface storms that required the submersing of the dome until the storms had passed. The weather-related arrivals and departures were carefully planned and executed to ensure the safety of the travelers and the integrity of the GaliPort dome and its platform. After quarantine was completed, the visitors could travel by tube or submersibles to the various UnderPod destinations based on their planned choices of the wide variety of entertainment and services available.

The bulk of the travelers came to ride in the underwater submarines and marvel at the freshwater coral castles, most of which rivaled the heights of Earth buildings covered with living plants in colors and sizes to take the breath away from the most discerning visitor. The sub tours were the most popular attraction for the photographers. These coral cities also appealed to the shallow water divers who needed to be pre-certified in a diving protocol on Poseidon. Certification from any other planet was not accepted. Diver's trips were usually longer and more expensive to include the dive certification requirement.

The planet had some very unique opportunities for the truly adventurous. It was claimed that in the ancient history of the planet, it had not been completely covered in water, but had land masses similar to that of the Earth planet, with buildings, civilizations, and commerce that had been transported across the freshwater oceans. The fabled history claimed that perhaps some catastrophic planetary shift or other unknown phenomenon had claimed the land masses with their cities and wealth of precious metals and gems which lay within the cavernous ruins. For a substantial fee, the adventurous divers could be transported to the ruins areas to search for the vast treasure vaults, if they could find them.

The advertising showed divers holding small gold plates covered with gems and shining metal coins. Treasure divers were not allowed to keep the artifacts they found. But they received credits for return trips and their names and photos were on display and available for sale in photo book volumes, in the museums of Poseidon. It was an honor to have your photo and story in the volumes of 'The Treasures of Poseidon'.

Roger Dalton and his friend Angel Witthouse, both from Earth Stoneybrook, Ireland, had their entire lives, read stories of treasure seekers and dreamed of being able to embark on a real treasure adventure one day. When Angel told his friend Roger that he had been diagnosed with a medical condition for which there was no solution, Roger decided that he must take Angel to Poseidon and mark that adventure off their bucket list. They had been together for so long, there was nothing he wouldn't do to share the precious remaining time with Angel, creating memories and experiencing the joy of life that remained.

Ireland had no GaliPort near them, so they would need to transport to either the CA Territories in the U.S.A. or St. Petersburg in Russia. They easily decided that the United States would be a great way to start their adventure. Of course, transport to the United States meant a three-day stop in New York City where they enjoyed taking photos of the Statue of Liberty and the iconic buildings of the Big Apple.

The stopover in New York City was an easy decision for Roger. He was an architect by trade and knew well the amazing history of the concrete jungle with its ever-evolving architecture throughout generations of innovation. Three days wouldn't be nearly long enough for him to explore the progression of the buildings, but this trip was for Angel.

Following the brief bite of the Big Apple, they continued on their journey to play in the casinos of Las Vegas which were often referred to as Lost Wages. Their week in Las Vegas was spent playing and sightseeing during the day while their evenings were dedicated, beside the virtual fireplace, to pouring over the many reviews and maps of the undersurface of the planet Poseidon.

The evening before their appointment, Angel discovered a small dot on one of the maps. It almost looked like a bad pixel in the tablet, but when they zoomed in closer and closer, they discovered that it was clearly not a blemish or flaw in the image, but 'something' similar to a tip of a spear above the surface of the water. They were both stunned but made notes of the coordinates of the 'dot' after which they proceeded searching supporting evidence of what may lie in the vicinity of the 'dot'. They spent the rest of the night searching radar and sonar records of the GPS located 'dot'. The sun rose despite their lack of sleep.

Finally, during their appointment process with I.O.T.A.A., it was explained that there would be more forms to fill out for the Treasure Hunting portion of their trip. The gentleman said the need for the insurance liability forms was necessary since there would be dive training on Poseidon. Life insurance was required because any time spent in the water without the protection of a submarine was, of course, subject to some risk.

They were happy to pay their fees and sign any forms needed to continue their bucket list adventure. The following day with completed decontamination procedures, Angel was first to GaliPort.

He watched as the Monitor counted down:

T minus 5...4...3...2...1

In what seemed like the blink of an eye the monitor displayed:

> **"Welcome to the planet Poseidon Mr. Angel Witthouse. Please step through the door to your right to begin your**

decontamination procedure. Have a nice
adventure Mr. Angel Witthouse."

Moments after Angel departed, Roger watched the same
countdown:

T minus 5...4...3...2...1

His next sight was the monitor displaying:

"Welcome to the planet Poseidon Mr.
Roger Dalton. Please step through the
door to your right to begin your
decontamination procedure. Have a nice
adventure, Mr. Roger Dalton."

When this second decontamination was complete, they
were not however whisked off to their UnderPod resort.
The travelers were notified that the presence of a storm
required that the GaliDome be submersed for a weather
period based on the activity of the storm. I.O.T.A.A.
regretted the inconvenience, but the travelers were assured
that The GaliDome was prepared to serve their needs
during this delay. Some of the travelers were distressed
about the delay but I.O.T.A.A. agents assured them that
their booked submersible and diving plans would be
upgraded to priority recipients of VIP treatment.

The delay was not an issue for Roger and Angel, it
provided more opportunity to continue their hunt plans
with even more current data. The material they had
searched on Earth has been baseline data – not considering
the possible weather-related shifting of the planet's floor.

Their dive training would start the following morning,
the theory portion was available electronically, but the pool
diving couldn't be done until they were able to transport to
the UnderPod resort. So, they slogged through the E-

lectures and took the tests following each module, as they waited for the end of the passing storm. After two days of storm delay, they were able to be transported to the UnderPod where they were told their pool training would begin first thing in the morning.

The dive training was not physically difficult. The educational process of the diving certification was somewhat long but interesting, in that the instructor enjoyed sharing both the real history of the planet as well as the embellished folklore. The actual dive training was easier than saltwater diving because the fresh water was not as buoyant as salt water. This lack of buoyancy reduced the amounts of burdensome weights needed for saltwater diving. Two days of lectures and diving finally yielded their certifications and a transport schedule for the following morning to their remote-selected GPS dive quadrant.

Upon arrival at the perimeter of the designated quadrant, the transport service dropped off a temporary PortaDome and its adventurers Roger and Angel. The PortaDome device was a portable piece of equipment that was reminiscent of a popup camper tent, but equipped with high energy portable food items, a disposable personal needs device, fresh drinking water, and an E-comm device to call for a departure, emergency assistance, or to provide temporary housing should the divers choose to take a break and revisit their dive location over the pre-paid five-day excursion. Not all dives required the temporary PortaDome service, but the distance of their chosen location demanded the service for their comfort and safety.

The evening before, they had met with other quadrant divers who would be going to various locations. Some discussed their reasons for their selected targets, while others were more secretive, wanting to ensure that they would not be sharing the treasures they expected to find. Roger and Angel were in the latter category, they were convinced that the 'dot' they had seen was missed by others

100

who may surely have done their own research.

* * *

Today was their adventure start day, with one last hug before donning the diving suits. The remainder of their gear would wait until they reached the quadrant. Once at their location and with the temporary PortaDome all set, Roger and Angel used AquaScooters to move them quickly from the PortaDome closer to the pre-programmed GPS location for their actual dive. The AquaScooters had their own inflatable 'parking' anchor allowing them to leave the AquaScooters when they got within visual distance of the 'city' they were seeking.

They saw foliage in extraordinary colors and magnificent in their sizes and shapes! Some were delicate looking, while others were menacing in their size and heaviness. They stopped their forward progress to take some initial photos, and slowly looked at each other then back at the outline before them. Although it had initially appeared to be just a moving clump of sea growth, now they could better see the outline beneath the foliage. It appeared to be an arm, sticking straight toward the surface.

Atop the arm, something else, a clenched hand. Holding what??? Was it a 'torch'? More pictures from further back and different angles. As they moved to get above the 'torch' their flippers disturbed the silt beneath them and suddenly, magically, they were able to see in the sand spikes, uniformly spaced spikes of metal shaped in an arc. It was like a halo stuck in the sand! The arc was higher in the middle as though standing on its side, "Yes!!" Squeaked Angel, "Look. It's like the head of an angel that has been buried standing up in the sand!"

Roger was confused as he looked at the 'angel' buried on the sea floor. Why would the angel be holding a torch up in the air and why would her halo be spikes and not the filmy circular halo like the paintings of angels or the Madonna. There was only one thing to do, they must move to the Angel and begin to free her from her silty sea bottom bondage.

Roger was suddenly interrupted from his reverie, as Angel said through the speaker. "We need to back up for a distance photo." Once framed in, it was clear by the proportion that what they were seeing was a plant-covered Miss Liberty! She was in front of what appeared to be the New York City skyline covered over with more plants!

Now they could see the 'spire' shape that was clearly seated atop the Empire State Building! They took photos to assist them to calibrate the distance from Miss Liberty to the city. There was no need for words now, they knew they must return to the PortaDome to spread the news of their find. Experts would need to be consulted. "How was this possible?" they thought. For both of them, this was the find of a lifetime.

The two returned to the AquaScooters and back to the PortaDome as quickly as possible. As they reviewed the video and photos they had taken out at the quadrant, they were now able to zoom in on the images. It quickly became clear that the form beneath the foliage was a mottled blue-green material, could it be stone or metal? There was no explanation they could think of why this planet, which was light-years away from Earth, could have at any point in history been host to the equivalent of planet Earth New York City complete with the Statue of Liberty.

They, finally exhausted from the stress, agreed to sleep before returning to the quadrant. The sleep time passed quickly as neither could shut off the mental skirmish swirling in their brains. After discussion regarding the return to the quadrant for further investigation, they knew they would need to penetrate the perimeter of the 'city' if they were going to find answers to the hundreds of questions they had. They poured over the photos and calculated that the 'spire' was from eight to thirteen kilometers from the torch. They discussed that the swim would be pretty strenuous, so it was probably best to make the trek using the AquaScooters and get as close as possible to the spire.

The plan to take both AquaScooters would give them the ability to return with treasure loaded on one. Now they had laid their plans for the upcoming trip to the interior of the city, their goal was to reach the Empire State Building which must surely be at the GPS location of the 'dot'. The AquaScooters would be employed to transport them closer to the 'dot'. From there, they speculated that they would be able to find access through the plant life to gain entry into a building. There was no thought given to the need to take an item that could be used as a weapon.

The AquaScooter trip took an hour to get them over the programmed GPS location. After anchor docking, they began their downward dive to the base of the spire.

Angel told Roger that he had found what might be an ingress into the building. Roger quickly came to his Angel and together they pulled back vegetation to reveal a door, which was more of an access panel than an actual door. The panel appeared to have been breached at some time before their arrival, so their combined effort yielded enough pressure to allow them access.

* * *

Day two of their adventure brought yet another unexpected shock. Inside the panel was a narrow metal staircase, overgrown, but navigable. When they reached the bottom level, the stairwell opened wider. Here were fewer plants, and piles of what appeared to be crushed breather tanks, recording equipment, and bones. Near the 'wall' was an object that was a smooth dull metallic color, perhaps 10 feet long and slightly tubular-shaped but tapered and flattened at each end. The object reminded Roger of a very large eel, but there was no indication it was alive or moving, even with the surrounding water movement. He took several still pictures of the object in addition to the debris scattered on the floor, then he began to film the video that would surely change his life.

Angel was at the bottom, pointing at the debris for perspective. As Roger resumed the recording, the eely shaped object before him slowly rolled on its side. Now the object folded itself in half, the middle of the now exposed creature swelled and opened into what must surely be a mouth. Roger called out to Angel and pointed in the direction of the eel creature. "LOOK!" he screamed through the breathing regulator's mouthpiece, as he tapped furiously on the metal tank to get Angel's attention.

Angel turned in the direction that Roger was furiously pointing toward only to see the 'mouth' growing and morphing. It began to sprout tendrils that seemed to grow out of the sides of the mouth opening which contained rows and rows of pointed teeth. Angel froze in time from the shock, as the metamorphosis continued, and the tentacles changed shape at the ends as they grew. The shapes on the ends quickly turned to crustacean-looking claws. More tentacles issued forth containing small razor-sharp hooks which reached out for Angel and began to tear at his flesh. Angel was being crushed and drawn into the still swelling 'mouth' of the creature right before Roger and his camera!! In what seemed to be a slow-motion eternity, there were audible crunches and screams from Angel as the creature crushed and swallowed him.

Roger had no idea how he got up that staircase, nor did he have any memory of swimming to one of the docked AquaScooters. He had no recollection of driving an AquaScooter back to the PortaDome or calling for the emergency pick up. I.O.T.A.A. decided that the safest protocol for such a case as this was to quarantine Roger, it may be necessary to assist him with a drug-induced memory adjustment. This type of accident had happened before. The creature only needed to eat once every six months. Adventurers were not permitted in this quadrant during the bi-annual feeding time when I.O.T.A.A. staff would normally deliver food from the bin. Perhaps the surface storm had disturbed the creature and caused the early need for food.

Even suffering the shock of seeing his partner eaten alive, Roger had somehow managed the presence of mind to send the travel photos to their Earth home before sending the SOS for assistance from the PortaDome. I.O.T.A.A. hadn't counted on him sending the photos and video contents via E-comm to himself back to his Earth Stoneybrook, Ireland address, which was being monitored by a friend, Ian Hunter.

When the Poseidon trip had been planned, Roger had also coordinated with Ian to collect the photos and video material. Ian was orchestrating a huge party for Roger and Angel which was going to be a welcome home celebration for them when they returned. Ian had photos and video of the departure from Ireland, pictures of the couple in the United States in the Big Apple, their laughing smiles in 'Lost Wages', and images of the coordinate map with the spire 'dot' sent while delayed during the storm. Ian knew all that they had been doing on this wonderful bucket list trip and had the most wonderful plans for their homecoming celebration. In his mind everything was wonderful until he saw the last installment of images, he had just opened...

I.O.T.A.A.

IAN HUNTER

Ian was a long-time friend of Roger and Angel. In his opinion, they were one of the most perfect couples he'd ever known. They had shared their disappointments and pains throughout life, with staunch resolve and strength despite much adversity. Their joy was visible to all people in their orbits and their optimism was infectious.

When Roger told Ian that Angel was terminal and shared the plan to fill the bucket list with memories, Ian was naturally supportive and helpful. Roger gave him the login and password scan to his accounts so that photos and E-comm descriptions of the adventure could be compiled and turned into photo journal collages and posters to be used to decorate the welcome home party. Ian was well known for his event planning, and he quickly dubbed the event, 'Bucket List Celebration of Love and Life'. He'd been compiling the guest list for days and was struggling to keep the number under 200. There would be the finest variety of cuisine and wines. The entertainment was booked, and he was now working on the decoration plans to best represent the event theme. He had buckets decorated with sparkling multicolored bling to hold the lager brews, bottles of wine, and champagne. Of course, heart-shaped bouquets of balloons would be floating everywhere. The streams and ponds would be tinted blue to match the water on Poseidon and there would be gigantic foliage complimenting the water areas. There would be planet-shaped candles floating in the waterfalls and ponds everywhere he could get the event property to put a pool, and large screens to run constant streaming video clips and photos of the guests of honor, taken throughout their adventures. The center of the ballroom would have a champagne tower, modeled after the New York Empire State Building, made of fluted glasses containing the bubbly champagne that would be rainbow colored because of the lighting beneath the glass pedestal tiers.

The invitations were posted and the R.S.V.P.'s were pouring in. Nobody in their right mind would miss an event organized and executed by Ian. All he had left to do was get the remaining videos and photos from Poseidon....

Ian poured himself a short snifter of brandy. He'd been working hard preparing for this event and the images he had just received should have been the most important of the trip – the images of the 'dot' which had been laboriously isolated and positioned. The only people in the universe who could possibly be more excited about these photos would have been Roger and Angel.

He chose to start with the still photo images which according to the timestamps were the first of this trip. Oh, happy faces preparing to leave the little PortaDome and then images of the AquaScooter trip to what appeared to be a huge forest of beautiful colored foliage. He would have large screen monitors everywhere running video loops! "*YES*," thought Ian, "*just as I've depicted in the decorations for the party!*"

More stills, dozens of the 'forest' same distance but at different angles. "*Why*", thought Ian, "*are they obsessed with underwater growth? Where is the 'dot' that they have been seeking?*"

Next photo, *"OH, further back,"* Ian realized. Now pictures of fingers pointing at different locations of the forest. Ian was a little bit disappointed in the focus of this forest. But then, one more photo and he could see their interest, it was the 'New York City Skyline' under the forest and in the foreground. It was the head and raised torch of Lady Liberty!! How in the world could this be? A skyline resembling one on earth. *"But the Lady Liberty?!?"* thought Ian as his head began to swim.

Next picture had a scribbled notation, there in the NYC skyline, an arrow pointing to the spire of something. There was a large circular dot with an arrow, and it was above one of the pointed buildings of the skyline. "Oh, my lord, it's the spire of the Empire State building!" Ian had blurted it out loud in his surprise. They had found their 'dot'!

Ian was so excited he quickly finished his brandy and went to the next time-stamped item, a document file where apparently, they had returned to the PortaDome to regroup for the following video stamped from the following day. Ian didn't want to read a document, he wanted pictures, but he took the time to read what Roger had written, a detailed description of the discovery of the Lady and the Skyline followed by their plans to return the following day to the 'dot', which they were now referring to as the ESBldg. Roger and Angel were not able to accurately jot down their excitement for the following day when they would return. Roger documented his calculations of distances between the Lady and the ESBldg and their plans to find a way to enter the building.

Ian decided that the video was going to require one more splash of brandy, well maybe two. The video was sporadic while they traveled over the sunken 'city' on their AquaScooters to reach the Empire State Building. Underwater, It was Angel filming as Roger breached an access panel near the top of the spire, then inside Roger took the camera and shot video of Angel descending a staircase. Ian was surprised that there was minimal foliage growth to speak of inside the spire. The video went off briefly during the descent and finally Angel was on the bottom level pointing at something on the floor. *"Is that litter?"*, thought Ian, *"No it is too big for litter. What the heck is that?"* Angel was clearly excited and pointing all over the floor as Roger tried to keep up with the directions.

Finally, Roger zoomed in, and Ian could see the debris was, what looked like crushed cylinders, and what was that??? A SKULL and pieces of bones!!! And over there as Angel pointed, more skulls, more debris... Suddenly, near the wall, a movement. The camera swung in the direction as did Angel who was now transfixed as the 'eel' thing transformed into some manner of monstrous creature which proceeded to devour Angel as the camera continued to witness the event. Roger must have dropped the camera because now the video was sort of sideways as Roger must have been trying to escape up the staircase. The camera had however been tethered to Roger's wrist and managed to depart the building with him. The creature was no longer framed in, only the blood floating and spreading in the water above the floor with its previously eaten visitor remains.

* * *

Roger was now in the protective custody of I.O.T.A.A., still on Poseidon, but sedated in a medical dome on a surface platform. His caretakers would GaliPort to Varmus to be joined by the unconscious Roger in a few minutes. There was a medivac waiting for both of them to transport to a very remote facility where Roger would be kept chemically comatose while the physicians performed the weeks of memory removal procedures.

There would be panel discussions to determine how much memory needed to be erased. The customer information indicated that Roger was a life partner of the victim Angel, so the team would need to do a considerable investigation to determine the extent of adjustment needed. Previous victims of accidents had for the most part been pairs where both adventurers had been eaten. There was no precedence for this situation and no protocol in place for such an accident as this one. The two caretakers, members of the staff from Poseidon, would GaliPort to Bastille-Cortez, with no explanation of where they were going nor why. There were no charging statutes or justice processes for these two. They didn't even know about the accidental feeding of an adventurer.

I.O.T.A.A. immediately suspended all adventure diving trips claiming unprecedented weather condition issues in the Poseidon atmosphere. Of course, refunds were provided for those travelers who were unable to enjoy their planned trips. After weeks of panel discussions, it was determined that Roger should remain in the current vegetative state for the rest of his natural life or until he was used as a test subject for research, either way – he was living dead. Neither Roger's caretakers nor I.O.T.A.A. knew that Ian Hunter, on Earth, owned photos and written documentation about the final adventure of Roger and Angel.

I.O.T.A.A.

IAN HUNTER — I.O.T.A.A. OFFICES, MANCHESTER, UK

It didn't take Ian more than a day to get a transport to Manchester UK where he stormed into the I.O.T.A.A. building to address the monitor on the desk:

"Please provide your identification."

He quickly showed his QR to be scanned.
On the monitor:

"Thank you, Mr. Ian Hunter. Our records do not indicate an appointment. Please state the purpose of your business."

"My business is an inquiry into the death and disappearance of my friends on the planet Poseidon."
Several minutes passed as Ian's temper began to grow. Then the monitor display updated:

"I'm sorry Mr. Ian Hunter, you have not

provided sufficient information for a response."

"My friends, Roger Dalton and Angel Witthouse from Stoneybrook, Ireland are missing."

More minutes passed, then on the monitor:

> **"I'm sorry Mr. Ian Hunter, Client travel is privileged information, our records do not show your name as a family member. A family member is welcome to schedule an appointment."**

Ian now began to get loud, his voice interrupting the unearthly quiet of the building, as people began to stop and look at the impending scene. "I AM family and I demand to speak with an I.O.T.A.A. representative immediately!"

On the monitor:

> **"Please re-enter your identification to determine your familial relationship."**

He raised his wrist one last time for a second scan and the message on the monitor updated:

> **"I am sorry Mr. Ian Hunter; your identification does not indicate a familial relationship. Please consider having a family member contact I.O.T.A.A. for an appointment. Thank you for your patience."**

Ian raised his walking stick with the intent to smash the monitor when a white light 'door' opened yielding a pair of menacing-looking security guards to escort him to an office.

"Ok", said Guard #1, "tell us how we can help you."

"I need to speak with an I.O.T.A.A. representative. I have two friends who went on vacation. One of them is now dead, the other missing. I want to know where the missing one is."

Guard #1 replied, "Were you notified by I.O.T.A.A. of a death or missing person?"

"NO, I need to speak with a representative!"

Guard #2, "If you weren't notified, how could you assume a death and missing person? Are they overdue for their returns?"

"No, they were not supposed to return until next week. I."

Guard #1 interrupted Ian, "Well then Mr. Hunter, let me give you a card. You can schedule an appointment for next week if your friends do not return at their scheduled time." He handed a card to Ian.

Ian, being incensed at having been turned away by the I.O.T.A.A. goon squad loudly said, "I need a piece of paper and a marker please."

Guard #2 complied, and Ian wrote:

I.O.T.A.A.,

Regarding the missing Roger Dalton,

I have video proof of your sea monster eating Angel Witthouse. If I am not contacted within 48 hours explaining the whereabouts of Roger Dalton, the video evidence of your flesh-eating creatures on Poseidon will be publicly and universally aired!

My contact information is in Roger Dalton's file.

Regards, Ian Hunter

Unfortunately, in his rage and intent to get a resolution with I.O.T.A.A., Ian had neglected to share the horrific documentation with anyone in Stoneybrook. Fifteen minutes later he received a message from I.O.T.A.A. stating that the travel arrangements were prepared for upload to his QR allowing him to immediately be transported to Poseidon where he would be met by Mr. Dalton to share their grief at the memorial service prepared for their friend, Angel Witthouse.

Ian watched the monitor:

T minus 5...4...3...2...1

"Welcome Mr. Ian Hunter to Varmus, Please step to the door on your right to be escorted to your decontamination area. Our deepest sympathies for your loss, Mr. Ian Hunter."

"VARMUS??? I was told I was going to Poseidon!!!!!" Screamed Ian.

He awoke in a test subject's cell.

BREANNA — MERCARI

Team Straight: Breanna, Apolonika, Tsu, and Cameron, were decontaminating at Hephaestus GaliPort in preparation to return to their desired planets. For the last 24 Earth hours Tsu had worked tirelessly hacking and programming. When they arrived on Mercari, they would know every step David Arthur took. His QR would block him from departing the Mercari GaliPort. He was now trapped, and Breanna would be coming for him.

The numbers of betting credits wagered across the universe could only be expressed in scientific notation. Fortunes were made and lost based on the extraordinary advertising claiming that the First Annual Colossal Hunt was to be the ultimate demonstration of masculine excellence. the hunters had been envied throughout the universe as the 'ultimate killing machines' while offspring of all races had, over the past month aspired to become hunters. The potential fame and fortune of future hunters were intoxicating to both male and female.

As the universal viewing audience cheered for the hunters in anticipation of the outcome of the hunt — reality set in. Just as the tides of the ocean crash to the shore and after the dreams and fantasies of the masses reached a crushing conclusion, so came the dismal and climactic defeat of those revered hunters.

CAMERON

By the time he was transported from Mercari to the GaliPort in Manchester, UK, his former business partner Doctor Tatiana Fedorov was already in custody awaiting trial for a laundry list of crimes. Tsu had collaborated with Cameron about the business ventures and went off with lightning speed to research and provide the legal proof that Cameron needed for the authorities on Earth to begin their charges against Tatiana. The charges included intent to commit murder in addition to a host of other crimes including lifeform and human trafficking out of TerraOra and Eros and drug trafficking. There was no doubt that Tatiana would spend the rest of her life in prison. Prison seemed a small price to pay for her desire to have him murdered, but the penalty would be determined by a court of law.

The financial cost of the crimes related to the business included substantial fines and restitutions. These penalties were sufficient to incentivize Cameron to divest the company holdings. It was evident that he would need to reinvent himself. The team had anticipated this possibility and planned for it. Cameron would rejoin the Team Straight on Mercari. DAE was so diverse and corrupt that there would be much work involved in sorting it out and reorganizing it into legitimate business conglomerates. The team felt it was good marketing to use 'Team Straight' in their branding because it became universally known over the five days of the hunt. Tsu seemed to be a bottomless pit of energy as he hacked and assembled data necessary to execute revenge on the people who had been responsible for sending Team Straight to the hunt.

* * *

Tatiana had a background in computer science with a doctorate in business. In addition to the lifeform trafficking, she had been involved in the hiring of architects and construction workers who had, seventeen years ago, been designing and building the domes, infrastructure, and security programs for the most secure prison planet in the universe. When Cameron and Tsu began to unpeel the onion of her ventures, they discovered a concentrated focus on the Bastille-Cortez prison planet security systems. It was ironic that her sentence would place her at BC for the rest of her life.

Tsu was a master of interpreting and reorganizing chaos, so he assured Cameron that even though his trip to Earth Manchester would be short, he would take Tatiana's information to Mercari and continue the investigation. He had already provided Cameron with the legal briefs to get the litigation ball rolling. After that he would be focused on unraveling the tangled mess of DAE on Mercari. That needed much work to determine what needed to be dissolved, saved, or reassembled. Breanna had David where she needed him, currently locked down in a service labor area of the city, where he could neither escape nor do harm. She let Tsu know that there was no rush.

APOLONIKA

Following the outrageous ending of the hunt, the Team Straight took the GaliPort to Mercari to plan their futures. Tsu and Cameron would be working to sort out the corrupt facets of David's business ventures in addition to litigation against Cameron's business partner back on Earth UK. Breanna knew those business concerns were complex, but logic would prevail in sorting those issues out. Apolonika was a personal concern as to where her future would lead her. The four members of Team Straight had yielded financial benefits from winning the hunt, so her financial security was not an issue.

King Apolonika had no real plan for her future. She had no marketable talents but decided that perhaps she could be valued back at the girl-child compound to assist those girls like her with no destiny other than destruction until such time that Breanna could try to make changes to the hunting planet concept.

Apolonika had been raised as a woman on TerraOra with no idea of who her parents were or from whence they came to be on TerraOra. Being raised in the compound afforded the girls little or no education or history about their families. The residents of the compound were the only family the orphaned girls knew, they had existed solely to await the time when they would be moved to other planets. The caretakers didn't tell the girls that their destinies would be from a list of destinations that would offer some level of slavery or death. In the rare case, there might be one's good fortune to be sold for domestic use where a girl might learn to cook or clean, but these opportunities were few and far between. Most planets had androids for domestic needs, so education was not on the 'to do' list when it came to preparing the girls. Apolonika had, because of her size, agility, and strength, been a special case where her talents were encouraged and trained. The caretakers expected that she would die in the hunt of Hephaestus, but they hoped that, with their encouragement to develop her physical attributes, she might have a chance to survive longer than a true female.

Breanna got to work on the computer searching to find Apolonika's parents. After exhaustive TerreOra records were searched, she discovered the names of the deceased parents and the fact that they had come to TerraOra from the Earth country of Lesotho. Lesotho is a mountainous, landlocked enclave surrounded by South Africa.

The enclave was originally inhabited by local tribes of hunter-gatherers called the Khoisan. Later in its history came the Bantu tribes and eventually the Sotho-Tswana people joined the area. By the time her parents were born, her blood line was Khoisan, Bantu, and Sotho-Tswana.

Armed with photos of the Lesotho people and the beauty of the mountains and waterfalls, Breanna was able to talk to Apolonika about the possibility of sending her to Earth where she could be part of her true African family. Of course, Mercari was an option to consider if she wanted to get educated and continue to be part of the new Team Straight Enterprises of Mercari operations.

Even with no formal education, Apolonika knew that

working for the new company would be a sociological challenge for her, and she thought that it would be nice to meet a real blood family if they would have her. If she had the confidence to get an education, perhaps she would be able to join Team Straight Enterprises of Mercari. She was only 17 years old and had plenty of time to carve her future path.

Further investigation and DNA analysis yielded information including the names of about 200 members of her family that still lived in the enclave. Breanna hired a tutor to teach Apolonika to read and write while she proceeded to contact the Earth Africa families. Of course, the families were all delighted to host or take in this orphaned member.

Apolonika was an apt student and writing was easy for her with the tutor encouraging her to chronicle her life in the girl-child compound. The tutor told Breanna, that this woman could easily become an author writing tales of the lives of the girl children of TerreOra if her education was continued on Earth. What a brilliant idea, Breanna should have thought of this, but agreed that the tutor should travel to Earth and continue the tutoring there. Breanna would make the financial arrangements for both of them in addition to funding their lodging and other necessities. The only thing left to do was to make sure that this was what Apolonika wanted. Breanna did not want her to feel like she was being pushed away from the only team she had ever known.

The GaliPort in Africa was located outside Johannesburg approximately 454 KM from Lesotho by vehicle. The trip could be made faster by transport or train, but Apolonika and her tutor Destin agreed that the overland route would be good to see and chronicle as they each embarked on new lives. The date set for the travel drew near bringing both excitement and apprehension. Breanna knew that this was an amazing opportunity for her and from the communication she'd had with the families, there would be months of visiting and stories shared with more love than anyone could ever hope for. In Breanna's research, she discovered the true gender of Apolonika. As awkward as this might be, it was only fair to share the information with her.

The week before the planned trip to Africa, Breanna sat down with Apolonika and explained what she'd learned about gender alteration and her understanding of the reason it had been done. She said her research indicated that this was rare but not isolated. Apolonika had seen the anatomy of the hunters and understood what she was missing. Breanna then felt like the hardest part of the discussion was yet to come, that if Apolonika chose to have gender reassignment done to make her more like a true female, there were procedures that could be arranged.

Apolonika's face lit up with joy! She said to Breanna, "How fortunate I am not to be burdened with the breasts that will sag and the bleed that comes with being born as a Queen! Breanna, you have made me a very happy King! You have brought me the best gift of knowledge, and I am indebted to you my dear Queen friend!". Breanna was extremely happy that she was able to find and share the information.

Destin would transport through in advance of Apolonika and be a face of familiarity upon her arrival. Cousins who lived in Johannesburg would be waiting when they were released from quarantine to show the city before wishing them farewell on their journey to Lesotho.

The cousins had plans for huge gatherings of second and third cousins and friends waiting eagerly to entertain and feed Miss A as she was dubbed even before her arrival. Miss A and Mr. Destin were taken shopping to ensure that they could have comfortable tribal clothing for their trip, and in just a few hours, Miss A looked like any other handsome African woman on the street.

The cousins were so proud to discover that she was in truth the famous King of the Team Straight. Many of the cousins preferred to refer to Miss A as King because they had seen her fame in the hunt. They had all seen the previews as well as the telecasts of the multi-day event, with no knowledge that this King of the hunt was actually a blood relative to them. The information about the hunt hadn't been shared by Breanna with the relatives. Apolonika would need to choose if she wanted to share that portion of her life story. It was best to come from the King rather than Breanna.

As Destin, Apolonika and the cousins walked the streets of Johannesburg, there began a chant that rose above the rooftops. "KING! KING! KING!" The chant began with a few and swelled as a tsunami pressing to the shore. She was surrounded by smiling black faces that chanted and raised their fists in the air as she had done on the final day of the hunt. Raising their faces to the sun, fists in the air, the chant went on and on KING STRAIGHT KING!!!!!

Miss A didn't need to initiate the story, she was easily recognized by all who saw her, and she wore her fame very well. She was cloaked in love, and she was home.

I.O.T.A.A.

DAVID ARTHUR

The first thing David did when he saw the image of the triumphant Breanna on the monitor, loudly inciting females to rise against dominance, was to tell his aide to book him to Earth GaliPort. When the request was instantly rejected, he knew he had lost some control, but he had no idea what terror lay before him. Breanna's plans to hunt David's movements were in place before the Hephaestus hunt was completed.

He would be herded to a small area of MetroCity on Mercari. His credit program was locked, forcing him to seek the limited list of lodging locations included in the predetermined credit program. Breanna had told Tsu that they needed control over where he could hide. With each day that passed his safety zone would be reduced. There was no army of enforcement necessary, only the ability to squeeze the area smaller, by disabling his credit with establishments providing lodging and food. She would be hunting him, not to inflict physical harm as he had planned for her, but for the satisfaction derived from the terror she would induce in him by constricting his power.

Mercari was one of the smallest human habitable planets

developed by I.O.T.A.A., but its design was to appeal to the wealthiest of businesspeople throughout the universe. Its climate most resembled Earth Hawaii with its tropical beaches and year-round consistent temperatures. It provided an atmosphere of comfort and relaxation for those business CEOs who had sufficient wealth and power to leave the management of their large corporations to underlings. They enjoyed the luxury and privacy available on the small planet populated with like-minded people of power. I.O.T.A.A. had strict policies in place to ensure ownership, occupancy criteria and standards were met.

These criteria would have prevented Breanna from living on Mercari if she hadn't already been married to David Arthur before his indictment and subsequent incarceration. Unfortunately for I.O.T.A.A., Breanna and her Team Straight had quickly discovered that much of the immoral and possibly illegal activity performed through DAE was done with full knowledge of Mercari's MetroCity. Under the circumstances, I.O.T.A.A. had advised the governing control of the city to look the other way when it came to Mrs. Arthur's residency status and her reorganization of DAE. Team Straight waded through DAE as the governing entities built a case to sentence David Arthur to life without parole on the prison planet Bastille-Cortez, as soon as he was located and convicted.

There were pockets in the city, the service workers' areas, that were impoverished living spaces. These areas were not desperately squalid locations but were markedly different from the opulent business areas of the cities. To the fugitive David, these areas seemed to be a living hell. Breanna squeezed David to ever smaller areas of the city where the poorest of poor service providers lived. She squeezed him by turning off more and more locations available to use his credit. He had lost over 20 pounds and often found himself needing to sleep in a beach house when he was suddenly turned out of a rental room as his credit was cut off to that establishment. He had tried a hundred ways to contact Breanna to beg her forgiveness, to beg her to at least let him GaliPort back to Earth where he would never be a bother to her again. But she squeezed him further, for fifty days she squeezed him closer to the most abject poverty. She wanted ten days of his life for every single one she had run for her own life during the hunts. She knew every beating he'd taken and every meal he'd stolen from a trash bin. He suffered greatly learning the life of squalor and personal loss. And finally, on day fifty, she let the police know where to find him so he might be convicted and sent to BC. In all the universe, David's conviction and sentencing gave new meaning to 'speedy trial'.

* * *

The DAE of David Arthur Enterprises that was once on the front of the building and all business letterheads and related items had been rebranded to bear the TSE of Team Straight Enterprises. The Team Straight executives and their aides met in a conference room to review all of the DAE issues needing resolution or attention.

Breanna started the meeting by asking Cameron for his discoveries of any DAE-related business. His former business partner Tatiana was in prison, but Cam had worked with Tsu to sort out the combined business efforts and any illegal activities affiliated with I.O.T.A.A.

"Well, as you know, my former partner was involved in a cornucopia of illegal activity, but the items related to I.O.T.A.A. are the things I will bring forward here. There are three main topics. Prey lifeform import trafficking on Hephaestus, which includes slavery and murder. Lifeform kidnapping and enslavement on Eros and hybrid lifeform trafficking and murder, also on Eros.

I have a report that itemizes the staggering number of

offenses, but she is in prison on BC now. We are left, however, with the development of solutions to prevent the illegal activities from continuing."

When Cameron's presentation was completed, Breanna turned to Tsu, "Thank you Cam, after Tsu gives us the DAE report, we will discuss the actions we need to take to divest DAE activities from TSE. Tsu? You're up!"

Tsu said, "You can call me Jack, it's the identity that freed me from the yoke of convention! The activities of DAE related to I.O.T.A.A. are as follows: On Ceres there is the manufacture and export of legally distilled products to multiple planets, export of produce from Ceres to TerreOra and export of grain products to other planets.

With TerreOra we have to deal with the hiring of butchers, purposed with processing humans for food. General lifeform trafficking, and murder with the purpose of being a food supply to multiple planets and lifeform trafficking to Eros for purpose of breeding stock i.e., slavery. Then there is bank and financial fraud where miners' funds were mismanaged by the DAE holding company and miners were denied the sending of monies to other planetary family entities. The miner's insurance policies with DAE holding company as primary beneficiaries. And finally, girl-child trafficking and murder.

Then we have Eros and though David was not directly involved with the trafficking or slavery on Eros, we need to discover what we can do to put an end to it.

And finally, Cheimon where there is the manufacture of the genetically modified protein for the winter planet. As a side note, this protein has both an addictive and extremely violent effect when eaten regularly."

Breanna took back the conversation, "Thanks Jack, I'm sure you have a volume of statistics, graphs, and charts, right?"

"Yes Ma'am", replied Jack with a smile.

She continued, "So now comes the hard part, as I see it,

we would be okay to keep and expand the Ceres distillation and farm products exports and rework the banking program on TerreOra for all the miners to benefit from their credits. Of course, the girl-child trafficking has already been temporarily closed. The compounds continue to house and care for the children as they await a resolution.

I believe the best solution for them will be what we did with Apolonika. Locate parents and families to reunite. TSE will need to consider an educational program for the girls awaiting adoption. We will need a tightly controlled process to closely scrutinize adoptive applicants and ensure the safety of the girl children until the compound is empty and dismantled. For the older ones, perhaps a variety of vocational training programs can be developed in addition to primary education. The funding for this education, adoption, and dismantling of the compound can be paid for from the stolen funds and insurance policies fraudulently acquired and held in DAE holdings.

Regarding Cheimon, Jack, is this protein still being used on the planet?"

Jack responded, "What I saw last week was a temporary ban on the use of the protein following the murder and felonious assault on multiple locals. Apparently, the local control is attempting to find a solution."

"Is, or was, DAE involved with the export or distribution?"

"No Breanna, only the concept. We are not at risk on this", replied Jack.

"AMEN!! We need to consider how to fix the things that we can, and I have an idea of how to make this happen. If we can get into the upcoming I.O.T.A.A. symposium, I can attempt to drive the panel groups to our logical conclusions for solutions. If I.O.T.A.A. rejects, I can threaten exposure. But of course, that strategy could backfire and make me a target. The question is how to get on the guest list? The fiftieth-year symposium is BIG and coming up in sixty days."

"Buy a seat!" said Cam.

"Cam, you can't just buy a seat ticket."

"Breanna, the seat is free if you are a stockholder. Jack, how much stock do we need to own to get a primary seat?"

"Already done! Breanna, you should get your invitation in forty-eight hours."

"Cam, you are a genius and Jack, you are truly a Jack-of-all-trades! Who's is going to stay on Mercari and who's going with me as an aide?"

Cam said, "I'll stay to continue with the girl compound process. There will be a need to import teachers and continue the familial searches. Jack should go with you because he's your 'Jack of all…' and he can ensure that there's no hijacking when you are ready to return to Mercari."

"Guys, if we don't pull this off, we will be marooned on Mercari."

Cam cracked a smile when he said, "Can't think of a nicer place to be marooned…."

Jack chimed in," Or better company…"

BASTILLE CORTEZ

Of all the planets upon which I.O.T.A.A. had business ventures, GaliPort, and GaliWorm locations, the one planet they struggled to develop was the one they named Bastille-Cortez, commonly referred to as BC. All planets had their share of criminals. Some of these convicts unfortunately were guilty of such heinous acts, that their presences needed to be maintained in a more secure manner than what was available on their home planets. With the construction of the GaliPort and GaliWorm transports throughout the universe, there was increasing pressure on I.O.T.A.A. to have a location dedicated to these baser lifeforms that had proven the need to be housed in highly secure facilities. Those criminals, ordered to be permanently incarcerated, were now transported to BC - the most secure prison in the universe.

The architecture and infrastructure of this planet were a challenge when housing needs were considered. Not all lifeforms were as easily adaptable to the human class planet environments selected to house these criminals. This diversity of environmental needs demanded separate prison community areas able to be environmentally controlled for the 'particular species' housing. I.O.T.A.A. was adept at the creation of dome centers, but the maintenance of the dome temperature controls was tedious in their creation and required artificial intelligence and droids to attend to them.

At least 90% of the prison population was completely isolated except for one BC hour each day. During the one hour, prisoners were allowed access to an outdoor running track. Each prisoner had his or her tracking and violation response unit embedded in their QR. If a prisoner got within ten feet of another, thus violating social distancing rules, the violation response would be activated immediately to alert security as it simultaneously disabled the violator. BC had been operational for approximately fifteen Earth years and there had never been a physical action that had not been successfully squelched within seconds of the attempt.

There was one non-AI representative to oversee each lifeform dome area. The overseers were not prevented from interacting with others, but as a security measure, their living quarters were separate life domes. Other than these, the planet was run by androids. All food preparation was planned, prepared, and distributed by AI or droids. The bio-attendees hired to manage the planet performed their duties from the safety of their personal domes, most often only leaving the planet when there was some physical impediment to prevent them from continuing to perform their job task, which was not much work at all. These jobs were very lonely positions, so much research went into the psychological profile evaluation during the job application process.

Food, consumables, and prisoner deliveries arriving from GaliWorm, or in the case of arriving prisoners from GaliPort, were picked up and delivered to the appropriate prison domes by the secure and well-protected droids. Prisoners arrived from the GaliPort in their organic jumpsuits. The port room was protected by droids awaiting the arrivals, to install cuffs on prisoners' ankles and wrists. Upon arrival, the monitor instructed the prisoner to step to a security wall through which they must insert first their wrists followed by their feet to receive the electronic distancing cuffs, which gave the prisoner just enough mobility to walk in very small steps while controlling the distance between prisoners. The planet was devoted to 'life in prison' and the sterility of social interaction was enough to incentivize a prisoner to wish they were dead but sufficiently unable to act on the desire.

Unlike prisons on Earth or other planets, there were no creature comforts, entertainment, or communication with other BC residents. It was effectively a solitary existence intended to last until the prisoner died. Prisoner's quarters had nothing that could be modified to be used as a tool or weapon. The beds were invisible gravity fields upon which a person could lie to sleep in their temperature-controlled soundproof environment. Personal needs were addressed with the use of a portable system provided as needed and removed when completed. Water was provided in sealed pouches which began to dissolve when opened, so the prisoner could not store extra water for any reason or use the pouch for any purpose. Their food was similarly packaged and consumed while the delivery droid waited for completion. They existed in complete isolation except for the one hour on the track. Verbal communication during this time would be met with a violation warning. Subsequent infractions warranted discontinuance of the free time. At some point in time, the prisoners managed to devise a sign language that was not noticed by the droid guards. They were programmed for their specific functions, but not to 'learn'.

The arrival protocol required that a prisoner meet with the overseer of their particular species. The Earth overseer was a man named Jim Rivers. The purposes of the initial meetings were to instruct the prisoner on the rules and consequences of infractions as they lived out their sentences on BC. The overseer, unfortunately for Tatiana, was antagonistic toward her because her file included her crimes related to the trafficking of infants. Jim Rivers had reason to believe that he had girl grandchildren who had been trafficked from the planet TerreOra. She knew that no overseer on this godforsaken planet could be bought with the credit caches she had on multiple planets, but she suggested to him, that with sufficient computer access and personal time away from her cell, she might be able to locate where the grand girl children had been placed. As a result, she was granted computer time.

One of the first things she did during her computer time was to access and upload her personal files from Manchester into an encrypted system on BC. That idiot former business partner of hers, Cameron Wells had not taken the time to access her files. He had been busy enjoying the fame he got for surviving the hunt. In her pretense to be searching for information about the Overseer's grandchildren, she came across information indicating that David Arthur was slated to GaliPort to BC. Of course, it was easy to explain the need for her to coordinate her effort with David Arthur because he was involved with the mining employment program on TerreOra, the very planet where the Overseer's girl grandchildren were trafficked. She convinced Mr. Rivers that David Arthur would be a necessary assistant in finding the children.

The overseer was merely a figurehead. He normally had little more than no interface with any prisoners once they were established in their cells until the time they died or were sick enough that a droid was unable to respond to the health issue. Tatiana knew that she would easily have free reign here until she hatched a plan to get off this god-forsaken planet. The use of a computer was against BC policy, but in this special circumstance where Tatiana would be presumably searching for information to locate the grandchild or grandchildren, the Overseer chose to qualify the infraction based on the greater good. He knew that the discovery of his personally motivated infraction would be the end of his career. But if this very knowledgeable prisoner was able to locate the children, he would be delighted to leave this job to spend the rest of his life elsewhere getting to know them.

Her next step was to make some adjustments to her tracker, violation recognition, and response alarm controls in her distancing cuffs. She deftly executed these feats in clear view of the computer illiterate overseer. She knew the location of four grandchildren within the first hour of her searching, but there was no need for him to know this. She earned more freedom on BC by providing tiny bits and clues to keep the overseer chasing his tail looking for the grandchildren.

David was now here to collaborate with her on the renovation of BC enterprise. Their sentences may be to stay on this rock for the rest of their lives, but they didn't have to do it penniless, and she believed that money talked. They would earn much more than they left Earth with. She knew she would be able to find a way off, with or without David Arthur, but having him around would help her with marketing a plan to I.O.T.A.A.

She had of course modified their QRs to ensure that they were 'at large' on the planet and quickly arranged access to a new dome location for their personal use and business strategizing. Their food was provided by droids as done for the overseers and life was very comfortable for them. They had no physical relationship as each knew the dominance of the other and neither had a desire to be submissive. David's personal taste was to have a thing of beauty with no will to do anything but adore him, naturally, he would be able to obtain this once they were free of this place. She considered suggesting a way to get Breanna to

BC, in cuffs, and perhaps have her vocal cords severed so that he could abuse her at will. But David had no desire to ever see Breanna's face again.

* * *

Another set of data she found particularly useful was the fact that the I.O.T.A.A. stockholders were unhappy about BC being red ink rather than an income asset. Stockholders do not like red ink and BC was no exception. The cost of feeding and occasional medical needs of the prisoners were considered negligible overhead for the I.O.T.A.A. stockholders, but at some point, they demanded that there needed to be a revenue-generating enterprise on the planet. The majority voting block was prepared to vote to close the incoming GaliPort to new prisoners.

Tatiana had quickly discovered this chink in the I.O.T.A.A. armor and knew the path she needed to take to attain their freedom. Having David there to market her proposals was merely a necessary evil. Her aggressiveness tended to put people off, so she had always needed to maintain a high-quality, smooth-talking marketer in the toolbox of human assets. She personally found his overly friendly manner and contrived pandering to be overbearing and frankly nauseating, but it was one of those bitter pills she knew she must endure until she was free of this planet.

She had the complete set of infrastructure and security systems for BC. She could have easily changed her QR to send her to any planet she wanted, but doing this would render her to be a fugitive from justice. No, she decided, she must leave the planet with the blessings of I.O.T.A.A., so the plan must be to obtain an audience with I.O.T.A.A. members or stockholders to make the presentation. It would have to be a combined event that included David, with David doing the selling. She could sell the Overseer, Jim Rivers, he was easy. He was a lonely man and her weeks of hints and suggestions about his heretofore unknown grandbabies made him the useful idiot to get them an audience with I.O.T.A.A. There would only be one chance for success. If David blew the presentation, her overseer would be replaced, and they would join the BC solitary confinement community for the rest of their lives.

Their presentation would include the varieties of money-making enterprises that could put Bastille-Cortez in black ink which should greatly please the stockholders. Could these enterprises be affected by some hired management from other planets? Well, yes, but since she and David had done the work developing the complete business plans, they were the most logical choices to run the credit earning projects. It would be his job to convince them of the reason why the two of them were best suited to managing the businesses.

David had his charts and graphs and prospectus documentation in well-done slide shows without providing the logistics. If I.O.T.A.A. chose to cut them out and put them in solitary, it would cost them a lot to hire business managers to reinvent the wheel. He had financial models and projections to show the staggering financial opportunities, and though he exuded a confidence that Tatiana didn't share, she had no option other than to give him the reins. She knew she was not a marketer. But before the meeting, she reminded him for the tenth time, that if he blew it, she would have him murdered the first time he went to the track.

David's presentation would outline the best of the best of their many ideas for making BC a profit center. Those topics included turning BC into a farming planet, adding Personal Services as a option for prisoners, operating a comm center for prisoners and medical research since the unfortunate events on Varmus and the resulting destruction of China and the Dongguan GaliPort. Each topic had a list of marketing opportunities or benefits, a list of requirements such as equipment or training, and a risk assessment with mitigations. The presentation was complete, detailed and thorough.

These were just a few of the opportunities that Tatiana and David discussed and developed into a marketing plan to present to I.O.T.A.A. if David was as good a marketeer as his reputation, it could mean their freedom, or at least hers as she had no feeling for him other than his contribution to that end.

The day of the presentation seemed to be years not months away, but on that day, David did a fantastic job with his charts, graphs and marketing finesse suggesting astronomical credit assets to come from a variety of enterprises. Finally, after three days of deliberations and answering questions, the I.O.T.A.A. panel agreed to the proposal. The proposal included name changes for both David and Tatiana and an office on Earth from which to conduct the businesses accepted from the proposal. I.O.T.A.A. agreed to the terms and provided the requested details as Tatiana and David had defined. Initial executions were to be done on Bastille-Cortez until such time that new CEOs could be prepared to take over the operations. David and Tatiana would have overseer housing and provisions. This was agreed upon and the contracts were drawn. Fourteen months later, the two criminals were scheduled for their GaliPort to CA Territories Earth.

For David, on the monitor:

T minus 5...4...3...2...1

And then, to his horror:

"Welcome Mr. Charles Vincent to Dongguan, Please step to the door on your right to be escorted to your decontamination area."

And for Tatiana, on the monitor:

T minus 5...4...3...2...1

Followed by:

> **"Welcome Miss Regan Avery to Dongguan, Please step to the door on your right to be escorted to your decontamination area."**

I.O.T.A.A. had made special provisions to reopen Dongguan GaliPort for these two. Things might have been different if only they had known that Breanna was now a major stockholder...

I.O.T.A.A.

APHRODITE

There wasn't a shortage of women in Ontario Canada, but Marcel Deauveax, Angelo Arcostin, and Ernest Bapsisto were three frat brothers, each with what they deemed discerning tastes in women. They had traveled extensively across Canada, France, and the United States in search of the most beautiful available women.

When after two years of disappointment and dissatisfaction, it came to their attention that Bastille-Cortez had been advertising opportunities for young single men to enjoy the escort programs on Planet Aphrodite. The advertisements claimed that this place was a mecca for the most beautiful females in the universe. The planet was home to the annual Miss Universe competition. According to other data, the planet required escorts who did not maintain their cosmetic excellence, to be returned to their own or other planets. The obligations were stringently outlined in legal documents to prevent compromising the reputation of the planet.

The application to visit also had strict requirements. Visitors must be single, temporarily sterilized, and certified free of diseases including dormant virus afflictions such as herpes. Other health requirements included medically approved cardio, liver, and kidney functions. There were insurance beneficiary requirements. Temporary insurance policies could be purchased at the time of booking through the BC processing agency, which was one on the list of opportunities for profit that Tatiana and David had secured for BC. The cost of the month-long visit was significant, but they were all single and financially comfortable. They decided that this trip was a necessity for the beginning of their new adult lives and careers.

Angelo was engaged to be married to a beautiful woman, but Marcel and Ernest convinced him that they needed to do this, that this trip would reinforce that their friend had found the perfect woman. They would think of this as a bachelor party on steroids!! As they filled out the applications, they were careful to ensure that none of them answered a question that could possibly eliminate them from qualifying to go on the trip. Angelo struggled when it came to marital status, he was engaged. The choices in the application were married, single, or other. He felt that engaged would fall under the 'other' category. But as the group reviewed each application, he was outnumbered and changed his answer to single. Medical testing was completed and the three received their acceptance with the departure date.

The decontamination process was extensive – but finally, their time at GaliPort was ready to go.

Monitor:

T minus 5…4…3…2…1

"Welcome to Planet Aphrodite, Mr. Marcel Deauveax. Please step to the door on your right to be escorted to your decontamination area."

Five minutes later:
Monitor:

> **T minus 5...4...3...2...1**

> "**Welcome to Planet Aphrodite, Mr. Angelo Arcostin. Please step to the door on your right to be escorted to your decontamination area.**"

Five minutes after Angelo:
Monitor:

> **T minus 5...4...3...2...1**

> "**Welcome to Planet Aphrodite, Mr. Ernest Bapsisto. Please step to the door on your right to be escorted to your decontamination area.**"

The three amigos would be sharing a quarantine suite for a week, but there was plenty to do as they waited. There were videos and brochures detailing the variety of entertainment to choose from upon completion of their Q-week. It was plain to see that this planet was everything it had been represented To be. Even as their meals arrived in clear synthetic polymer, the presentations were impeccable and delivered by a variety of extraordinarily beautiful delivery women. There were no menus to select food, but everything that arrived was different from anything they had ever eaten on Earth, and it had been perfectly prepared by the finest culinary expertise. As they finally got their quarantine release, they could barely wait to move to their resort, they had each already reserved their choice of escorts.

The following week was days and nights spent exploring

the beauty of the planet and the escorts, at times with only one escort, other times, with multiples. The men had no time to discuss their individual pleasures, of which there were many. By the end of the week, all three were ready for a brief time to share their explorations and conquests. This was a plan they had made upon their arrival at the resort.

Marcel and Ernest met for dinner on the appointed day and time, but Angelo was not there. The two agreed that Angelo must surely have more stamina than they did since he neglected to take the weekend off, as previously agreed. So, they left a message for his room service delivery that they should meet the following evening at 5PM for supper at a designated location.

The following evening at 5PM, Angelo was still not present, and neither was Ernest. So, Marcel returned to his room a second night, alone and hungry. He called his favorite escort, Deidre, to see if she would share dinner with him. She said of course, but she would need to bring a couple of friends with whom she had dinner plans. She suggested that they would cook for him at his resort room if he was feeling strong enough to entertain them before dinner was served.

Marcel considered that he was too tired for one woman, but now the prospect of three beautiful women magically reinvigorated his libido! "Of course, I would be delighted to entertain you and your friends!", and they set a time.

He set up glasses of sparkling wine and plates of fruit before the ladies arrived. His Deidre brought in her stunning friends and quickly gave him a small pill which she whispered would ensure his endurance. The three nibbled on fruit and drank wine as they waited for the little pill to work. It didn't take long to act and as he entertained the ladies, they took turns returning to the kitchen which was emanating the most wonderful smells of dinner. After he had satisfied their entertainment needs, they returned to the kitchen area to eat. The food was delicious, and he asked what this first item was that he had thoroughly enjoyed. Escort Arietta said, "Oh that was my favorite 'Kidney Ernesto'…"

And he turned to Escort De'Lecatte and asked, "What is this dish you prepared? It was also amazing!"

She slyly smiled and said, "That was my favorite, 'Liver Angelorio'."

He neglected to notice the sizzling pans waiting to cook the final course. Nor was he aware that the two escorts were shape-changing, they were no longer beautiful, but rather slithering creatures with tentacles and far too many teeth in drooling mouths waiting to consume the final course. Still oblivious to the innuendos, he turned to his darling Deidra and said, "My sweet Deidra, did you not prepare your favorite for us to share?"

Deidra smiled and said, "My dearest visitor, You are my favorite, I shall call you Liver Marcel…"

I.O.T.A.A.

CHEIMON

Cheimon was a planet of perpetual winter, named for the Greek god of the winter season. The idea of escaping the overpopulated Earth was one of the attractions to this planet. It provided full-time sunlight. The distance of the suns was insufficient to overcome the frozen internal core of the planet which is why it was constantly the winter planet. As with most I.O.T.A.A. developed planets, dome surface living was comfortable.

The planet was especially attractive to those winter sports competitors, and DAE had developed a large variety of competition class training and event centers for skaters, skiers, and winter sports enthusiasts. As with all resort or training locations, there were many residential service provider employment opportunities available as well. It was a lucrative planet for all walks of life.

David had hired an army of agricultural scientists to ensure that the food supply was managed in commercial-grade hydroponic domes to avoid the cost of importing produce. There were also commercial fish hatcheries and aquariums for the protein provisions. The red meat protein source was fortunately unknown to the visitor community.

The meat protein had posed more of a challenge. Interplanetary groups were able to make suggestions for red protein which the Cheimon teams tried importing. The initial attempts to transport livestock and breeding pairs of red meat animals were not particularly successful and they quickly discovered that the percentage of successful transport was a diminished return on investment. David's group knew of other protein solutions used on TerreOra and Poseidon, but these solutions were small volumes compared to larger four-legged animals. So, he went to the scientists of Varmus for a solution.

The Varmus scientists soon discovered that the natural growth period of mammals was too time consuming and not suited to the Cheimon winter environment, so they developed a hormonal treatment that would allow the protein mammals to experience accelerated growth thus reducing the amount of time and space normally devoted to raising the animals.

Once the testing and intense hormone program was developed, David quickly imported some incubators from Eros to begin the breeding program. The animals were selected by their ability to endure the cold weather. They would be protected creatures on the planet, but he didn't want the cost of dome housing or the animal's feedlots. Although the animals' growth was accelerated by the hormones, David was not happy with the rate of growth, so he ordered a doubling of the hormone treatments.

The herds began to grow substantially through accelerated breeding and Cheimon was soon able to add large platters of red protein which pleased the athletes greatly. On previous visits to the planet, eating fish and produce had often resulted in weight losses for the athletes. With the new and improved menus, the athletes maintained their competition weights.

The marketing for Cheimon resorts and training centers boasted the four diamond slopes which attracted experienced, amateurs, and professional competitors. There were training centers for skaters including speed and figure skating arenas as well as separate ice hockey arenas. The gymnasium complex was a city unto itself. The service job opportunities were many and quickly filled by the importation of a variety of employees drawn from overpopulated and underemployed planets. There were premier medical facilities and focused sports medicine, physical therapy providers, and nutritionists who were available around the clock.

No different from other planets with large populations, there came the providers of the baser service provisions for hire. Male and female prostitution was available. Both were subject to controlled taxation and regular medical testing. Solicitation was not allowed from the streets but required to be controlled by appointment to ensure the safety of both the providers and clients. The appointment scheduling ensured that the controllers got their tax credits.

Babs, Boogie, and Sugar had saved and pooled their credits on Earth to start their own business on Cheimon. They were in their twenties but looked much younger so they were in high demand as long as they could keep their 'little girl' looks. They managed to get a sweet apartment and built their killer marketing strategy to create a lucrative business that became well known to the coaches of the gymnasium complex.

Berto, Chaz, and Woodie were roomies in the Prolympic housing facility. Berto was from Italy, Chaz from France, and Woodie from the United States. They would be competing against each other next year in the winter Olympics on Earth Europe, but they had become friends here on Cheimon, competing on the slopes and in the gym. They had been here for eight months consuming great quantities of the large steaks with each meal. Their muscle mass indicators soared as the intensity of their workouts increased exponentially. They seemed to be obsessed with the weights and measurements. Other competitors were getting stronger and bulkier also, but the trio was focused on their personal competition. The obsession to be stronger than each other reached a fever pitch and began to lean toward hostility as one boasted of recently achieved higher numbers than the others.

One particular Friday, after number logging, Berto and Chaz began to throw punches. Woodie tried to intercede but got drawn into the fight which needed to be stopped by the gymnasium manager. Erik was a large Russian who was known for taking physical action to control such situations. All three competitors sustained minor but visible injuries. Erik sat them down in the office.

"Ok guys, this isn't working here in my gym. You all know that I don't tolerate this kind of crap in here." There was no response from the trio. "I think you guys need to take a break from working out for a day or two. There is life beyond the slopes and the gym. So let me ask you, when was the last time you had a piece of ass?"

No answers

"Berto?" No answer.

"Chaz?" No answer.

"Woodie, You MUST have something going on?"

Woodie responded, "Coach Erik, we came here to prepare for Olympics, there's no 'pussy competition' right?" The other two couldn't suppress a chuckle.

"Well," said Erik, "this weekend there is. I'm going to schedule some girls I know about. Your workout this weekend is with the girls. I don't want to see ANY of you till Monday 0900 and you better come back with better attitudes, or I'll throw your asses out of my gym!"

But on Monday 0900, the three were not in the gym, they were in jail. Babs, Boogie, and Sugar were in the hospital. None of the girls would ever look like little girls again and the doctors doubted if any of them could ever be capable of conception while Sugar might never walk again.

Erik would be meeting with the nutritionists as soon as the guys' hormone testing was completed. He'd seen the increased aggression over the months since the food got better on this planet, he sure as hell hoped this incident didn't get back to I.O.T.A.A. management.

I.O.T.A.A.

TEAM STRAIGHT

They had planned the Symposium strategy on Mercari over the last few weeks toiling long hours assembling data to be used as ammunition when they got to the committee seats. Breanna knew she wasn't the businessperson that David had been, but she had learned a lot from observation, and she had a survival strategy second to none. So, as they had done before the hunt, they prepared both defense and offense strategies to ensure their financial strategies were more attractive than the immoral activities that had been executed for years.

She and Jack must convince the members of teams from multiple planets that a strategic shift to the Team Straight suggested moral activities would bring a higher return on investment for I.O.T.A.A. stockholders. Their plan for Ceres was to export Cerestini along with other distilled products and raw grains to other planets in the I.O.T.A.A. universe. Jack had assembled a volume of statistics, charts, and graphs, with projected models to demonstrate the wisdom of the proposed changes for Ceres. This would be their lowest priority and time expenditure in the committee meetings.

For Cheimon the only issue the team had discovered was with the genetically modified growth hormones in the protein food. The charts indicated the exponential rates of addiction and violent crime resulting from the growth hormone modified protein — GHMP. Though the discontinued use of GHMP would cause food sources to take longer to mature, the slight increase in overhead could be offset by increasing the herd feeding and breeding activities on the planet. The team had a projection model which identified the point when the feeding production modification overhead cost would shift to put the planet back in the black ink while staying within the law. This would be the 2nd lowest priority and time expenditure of the committee meetings.

On TerraOra, Team Straight had a temporary restraint order preventing the continued activity of the girl-child compound operation and all trafficking and butchering. They were also in the process of revision of the banking and insurance programs on the planet. These changes were indeed revenue loss to I.O.T.A.A.

Jack had a model that included the employment of artificial intelligence labor which could effectively increase production to sufficiently offset the inhumane and illegal practices that would soon be permanently disabled. This committee would be a passionate and high priority use of Breanna's time. They had planned that at the time of this meeting, she would be including a visitor aide from Earth Africa. King Apolonika would be a surprise visitor to this committee meeting to speak eloquently about the victimhood of the girl-child compound. She had been well-prepared by her tutor, Destin, for this presentation and Breanna knew that her involvement would be instrumental to the permanent removal of the operation from TerreOra.

As to Hephaestus and Eros, Breanna and Cameron had previously advised I.O.T.A.A. that if these breeding and trafficking activities were not immediately discontinued, the evidence would be disseminated throughout the universe and there would be recommendations issued to all planets to boycott any travel to them. She had warned that the Team Straight, now universal 'rock stars', would begin a devastating campaign to crush tourism to those two planets, and if that wasn't enough, others would follow.

The symposium panel's effort was to reconfigure the use of most of Hephaestus for open tourism while keeping the hunt area secure for hunters of the Swalk. Jack had tracked the history of the Swalk and discovered that they were not native to the hunting planet of Hephaestus, so I.O.T.A.A. could decide if these animals would continue to breed on the planet for hunt purposes or eliminated by controlled hunts until such time that the hunt areas could be repopulated with less dangerous creatures and thus more tourist-friendly rain forest visitation, or possible botanist research.

Of course, I.O.T.A.A. was eager to comply and quickly put a halt to the hybrid breeding program on Eros and simultaneously assisted in the cooperative effort to reunite the residents of the girl-child compound of TerreOra with family members when a family could be identified.

Lastly for now, their plan for Poseidon, if they had time to be involved on a panel for this planet, would be to block all travel and remove all residential staff until scientists were able to evaluate the future safety of the planet. Jack had found very secret information about the existence of the Neumok creatures, the feeding program, and memory reassignments of divers who survived Neumok incidents on the planet. If they were not involved with the planning for this planet, Team Straight might need to demand a Symposium on Mercari to discuss Poseidon and other planets that seem to each have their unique issues that neither David nor Tatiana had been involved with.

As prepared as they were on the first hunt day on Hephaestus, Breanna and Jack were well-prepared to sit in on as many possible panels to get I.O.T.A.A. on the right side of justice. For them it was a new beginning and as their name implied, they were going to set the record Straight.

THE I.O.T.A.A. CONSORTIUM'S FINAL ANALYSIS

"Ladies and gentlemen, I know that many of you have been to our annual meetings to discuss the progress of the I.O.T.A.A. Planetary experiment. Today, however, should be to all present, monumental, as we have reached the fifty-year anniversary of the GaliPort trial system!

Beginning today and throughout the coming week, it is incumbent upon all of us to review and evaluate the possible changes or improvements as we learn of the many successes and possible mistakes of the past fifty years.

The esteemed guests I see before me are a collection of scientists, stockholders, sociologists, and business analysts. Oh, and speaking of lawyers: Why don't lawyers go to the beach? Anyone??" There was a pause and then the Director proceeded, "Cats keep trying to bury them!!!! Ha, ha, ha, ha, uh, sorry about that, my wife told me I needed to make a joke.

But returning to the reason we are here. You will find

before you a module containing the complete compilation of the data separated by planet. We have asked you to spend the next 48 hours reviewing this data in preparation for subsequent team panel evaluations and discussions. Your data module will have on the first page the names of your team members and their contact information. I will ask Miss Teri Alonzo to put on the monitor a brief overview of the issues before us."

Teri introduced herself and presented a graphic which showed the complete planetary collection in I.O.T.A.A.'s universe. She advised there would be a sub-committee assigned to each planet and that each sub-committee would have a dedicated data analyst to gather more details as needed and that each representative would be allowed to have their personal staff participate. A committee member's personal staff could sit in on any number of other sub-committees of interest to their respective planet to gather data and ask questions. This aided in ensuring transparency.

Once Teri was finished the various members of sub-committees were excused to review and deliberate on their assigned planet. Teri was the master scheduler and made sure that Breanna and Jack had presentation time for each of the Team Straight planets of interest where they could present and work to convince the sub-committees to heed their advice.

At the end of the multi-day sub-committee planet reviews the Symposium was wrapping up. All sub-committee reports were published, and each gave a summary of their analysis and the outcomes which were the future plans for their respective planet assignments. Then it was time for the final wrap-up and Teri led that.

"Thank you all for the amazing success your teams have brought to the symposium this week. A tremendous amount of analysis, review and planning has taken place and the I.O.T.A.A. would like to extend our greatest accolades to you all. We have plans for the future and they are looking bright! Before we officially close the session, there is one last order of business we ask your attention to. At this time, I would like to introduce to you our newest primary stockholder, Breanna Arthur and her esteemed guest.

Breanna Arthur and Team Straight have rebuilt and re-branded the failed David Arthur Enterprises. Ms. Breanna Arthur, as the head of the new Team Straight organization, has been instrumental in identifying a variety of challenges on Ceres, TerreOra, Cheimon, Poseidon, Eros, and Hephaestus, all within I.O.T.A.A. auspices. Team Straight has presented to the various sub-committees that were dedicated to these planets and is presently devising and incorporating many of the solutions to improve them and develop best practices for future additions to the I.O.T.A.A. Megaplex. I.O.T.A.A. is extremely pleased to have Ms. Arthur and her team intimately involved in the process of identifying and bringing possible solutions in which you have all been involved this week. Please join I.O.T.A.A. in a round of applause as I invite your attention to Ms. Breanna Arthur and The King – Apolonika of Team Straight!"

Both women stepped to the podium, to raucously loud cheers and applause, but Breanna stepped to the side after raising the microphone to accommodate the King.

King Apolonika began, "Thank you for your indulgence as I briefly share my personal experience of victimhood resulting from being born on the Planet TerreOra. I was born to become one of the many unfortunates raised in the girl-child Compound of the planet. My fetal misdiagnosis of gender condemned me to castration, an unwritten policy to avoid discovery of the program. As an orphan of the girl child compound, I was raised as a female, but the lack of specific female biology prevented my designation to be, at the time of puberty, shipped to Eros for breeding purposes. The remaining options were the feedlots of TerraOra or the hunt prey bin of Hephaestus. Perhaps it was my blessing to be misdiagnosed which is the reason I did not become a slave of the mining program there.

It is my most sincere hope that I.O.T.A.A. will discontinue the enslavement practices perpetrated against women. There is no amount of credit in the universe to provide reparation for the theft of a lifeform or its use as a financial asset to be milked like the teats of a cow until the milk is dried and gone. Thank you for hearing my humble plea to replace injustice with righteous freedom which all lifeforms deserve."

And she gracefully raised her chin and her hand to the air to proclaim victory as she had at the end of the hunt. As she stood, so did the audience who also raised their hands in silent support as the tears rained down on their faces at the knowledge that they would no longer be a party to the former injustice. Breanna stepped to the podium beside the Apolonika, as she raised her hands in the victory salute, there was no need for her to speak; The King had conveyed the message succinctly. Teri, with tears in her eyes, joined the two at the podium.

"Thank you, ladies and gentlemen of the planet panels, for your valuable input. Corporate I.O.T.A.A. will compile all materials and recommendations for consideration and implementation. It is our sincere hope that we will see many of you next year after we have acted on the fruits of your labor here this week. I'm not much on speeches, so I leave you a bit of wisdom as you depart. The fate of the many rests on the shoulders of the few. May we experience the greatest success in our endeavors to make the I.O.T.A.A. Megaplex bigger, better and more beautiful."

'Never underestimate the power of a talented group of angry people with a mission to conquer evil.'

And so, it was the beginning of a new and improved I.O.T.A.A.

EPILOGUE

The conclusions and recommendations, spear-headed by Team Straight, were being executed with blazing speed and efficiency in the effort to rescue I.O.T.A.A. from the corruption that had begun to devour it from within. A new and better future was in store for the conglomerate and their many clients.

Unfortunately, some cases were beyond rescue. Ian Hunter and Roger Dalton had undergone memory reassignment to remove the pain of their loss of Angel Witthouse and eliminate the risk of their knowledge of his end from ever harming I.O.T.A.A. Neither would remember what they had seen, or how Angel had left them. Roger would only mourn the loss of a friend and partner. Ian's fate on Varmus was yet to be determined.

But others formed rays of hope. Angie and James Drummond were fortunate to be liberated from their personal hells, Neither had witnessed the hybrid lifeforms Angie had borne. They have been reunited and continue the dream of raising a family on Eros.

"The Devil doesn't come dressed in a red cape and pointy horns. He comes as everything you've ever wished for."

Tucker Max

I.O.T.A.A.

ABOUT THE AUTHOR

A big-city girl living in small-town Idaho, Maryellen Hunter is an avid reader turned writer with a passion for science fiction and intrigue. Her life's travels and experiences combined with the joy of meeting and conversing with people of all types have provided the seeds to create unique characters and situations.

Her writing style is designed to stimulate the imaginations of her readers as she lays trails of breadcrumbs to assist them to be a part of the creative process.

Her characters' personalities will become as personal to you as they were to her in her writing process.

She began writing after a lifetime of reading.

Today she struggles with vision loss due to Age Related Macular Degeneration (wet AMD) but continues to push forward and share her vivid imagination through her words.

I.O.T.A.A.

OTHER BOOKS
BY
MARYELLEN HUNTER

Book 1 – DECOMMISSIONED
The discovery
The fictional discovery of a viral bioweapon
Could it be that the 'cure' is the real weapon?

Book 2 – SAVIOR UNIT
The recovery
Civilization fights back after the truth is revealed.

Book 3 – DECOMMISSIONED CHINA
The retribution

The prophetic Decommissioned Trilogy was written 2 years
before the advent of Covid19
(warning: adult content)

ZORBECK
Whether by accident or design, the arrival of the Zorbeck,
a snail the size of a small car, is dining its way across the
country.
An army of misfits chases the Zorbecks across the country
in an attempt to stop their foraging.
Zorbeck is a tale that will keep you laughing.

SWIMMERS
This post-pandemic story is filled with corruption,
as the side effects of the Covid vaccines have rendered
large portions of the world population to be at risk of
extinction.
Never let a tragedy go to waste!!

TOMOT
Is a fictional story of a Native American girl who has power
over time, given by her alien father's civilization.
Follow Lily as she learns to use her power and seek the
knowledge of the star people.

THE CONSUMMATE IRONY OF TIME
In this book of short stories, you will meet the macabre,
invest in the imagination, and ponder the possibilities, as
you loathe or laugh at the irony of the inevitable boundaries
of time.